W. S. COOK

J. J. Marric

GIDEON'S POWER

HARPER & ROW, PUBLISHERS

NEW YORK AND EVANSTON

A Joan Kahn–Harper Novel of Suspense

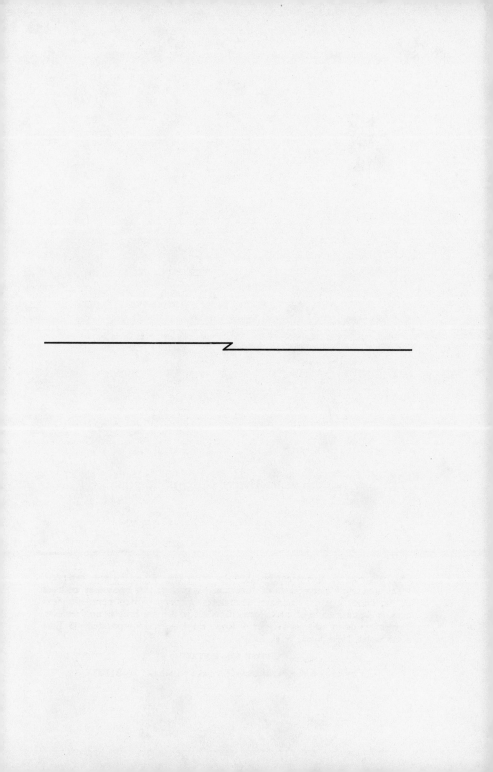

1 *The Big Smoke*

George Gideon glanced into his driving mirror, put out the left-hand indicator, and pulled his big, old-fashioned car to the side of the road. Ahead of him a cumbersome timber truck was standing; beyond that lay Battersea Bridge. As he got out of the car and stood up, he could see much more—the silvery surface of the Thames; two convoys of barges drawn slowly by a lighter, the engine of which sounded clear and deliberate across the water; Battersea Park in one direction; a huddle of old, time-darkened buildings on the other. Although he saw and was aware of these things, his gaze was concentrated on the great stacks of the Battersea Power Station and the huge, rolling billows of smoke which came out of each. It was a curious color, a blend of white, gray, and black gradually fading until, hundreds of feet in the air, it was lost against the pale, misted sky, dispersing only to fall soft as snow and dark as soot onto the roofs, the streets, the walls of London.

Gideon reached the parapet of the Chelsea Embankment.

The driver of the parked truck was also by the parapet, paper pack of sandwiches in one hand, thermos flask of tea or coffee in the other, alternately chewing and drinking. Cars and lorries swished by behind them and some sped over the bridge. But Gideon's attention was on the power station, a symbol of the power of London.

Across the river, in that massive building which had withstood Nazi bombing with high explosive and fire bombs,

1

there had been sabotage early that morning—not substantial, not alarming, and yet enough to worry him.

He was not easily worried, so much of his life was trouble —his working life, at least. He was Commander George Gideon, the chief executive of the Criminal Investigation Department of the Metropolitan Police, responsible for every one of the 8,000-odd detectives in London, and responsible for fighting every kind of crime which London harbored. Crime went on, day in, day out, in unending variety—most of it petty, although in the aggregate serious enough. Much of it was organized by men of great ability, planned and executed like a military operation, but by far the greater part was haphazard, conceived and committed by men who, wanting nothing but a comfortable living, had decided that the easiest way was by breaking the law.

The law-breaking affected everyone.

It affected people in their homes and in their shops and in their factories. It touched the old and the young, the white and the black, the rich and the poor. A single crime, committed without thought by one man, could affect the lives of dozens, even hundreds; and could do many people great harm. London, partly through Gideon, was geared to fight crime on a large scale, and he was sensitive to every aspect of it. Particularly so to any form of crime in industry.

There were, of course, variations, but industrial crime fell mainly into a pattern. There was pilfering on a large or a small scale; bold theft; vandalism. There was the careless crime, such as the breaking of the Factory Acts regulations or parking and drinking laws, and there were embezzlement and fraud. From time to time also, there was sabotage, usually against one firm. There could be several motives for this. A manufacturer might be getting ahead of an unscrupulous competitor, or a man or group of men might have some personal feud against individuals or management. Occasionally sabotage arose out of labor disputes, or had a political significance. Whatever the cause, it was usually possible to trace the culprits.

Recently, over a period of two or three months, there had been reports of sabotage in power stations which served heavy industries using a lot of power, but neither reason nor perpetrator could be found. In the past week, there had been several such reports, and this morning's incident had been more serious than most. A transformer, sending out electricity to one of London's densely populated suburbs, had been damaged with a corrosive acid, which had been put into a plastic, acid-resisting oil can. The machine-minder who had actually used the acid had not known what was in the can. The report quoted the department manager as saying that he was "above suspicion." Gideon was always skeptical of such claims, but in this case what he had learned from A.B. Division suggested that it was probably true. If it was, then someone unknown had filled the can and left it for another to use unwittingly.

The incident had caused a blackout over a sixteenth of London, delaying trains, bringing factories and docks to a standstill, causing risk to life in hospitals, and, in all, making half a million people suffer to a greater or lesser degree.

That was what worried Gideon.

It could happen again, and on an even larger scale. It could disrupt the whole of London, and such disruption could lead to disaster. These were difficult and tense days for London, the home of a third of Britain's industry, particularly those industries which produced consumer goods. It was easy to forget that—as easy to forget that export orders could be seriously affected at a time when Britain had never needed greater productivity or more export markets. So this was not simply a matter of crimes to be stopped and criminals caught; it went much deeper.

The smoke still billowed. Two more convoys of barges came into sight, fully laden, and then an empty one came along from the other direction. The wake from all of them caused a gentle, lazy swell. Swans appeared on the river near the lunching truck driver, and several ducks, and on the parapet close to him were half a dozen pigeons. The truck driver was a man in his middle forties, rather small, wearing a faded blue coverall and—unexpectedly—brown sandals. He made clucking noises to the pigeons, as if imitating their call. Two small boys appeared, out of nowhere, to watch.

Innocence, thought Gideon; simple innocence.

He remembered a notorious shoplifter who, whenever he was out of prison, spent his leisure time in feeding the pigeons which flocked near some of London's biggest buildings. The children one might judge fairly accurately to be innocent, but the man—there was simply no way of even guessing what was going on in his mind. That lorryload of timber, for instance, could be stolen.

Gideon half laughed at himself, turned, and nearly bumped into a young couple walking by.

"I'm sorry."

The girl was fair and pretty.

"That's all right," she said, almost gaily.

The man had rugged features and fair, curly hair. He simply nodded, and seemed to grip the girl's arm protectively. Gideon crossed to his car. It was after six o'clock on a September evening, and in a little more than an hour dark would begin to fall. There would then be a different shift working at the power station, and it was quite possible that the saboteur would be back on duty. The thought of going across to see for himself was tempting, but Gideon resisted it. Power station security men as well as Divisional and Yard men had already been drafted in; if the man tried any more tricks, he would almost certainly be caught tonight.

But would it be repeated?

It was the first incident actually inside one of London's twenty-three powerhouses, and quite possibly there would be no more. Already a number of the best men at the Yard had shown they did not connect this with the sabotage that had occurred at some transformers and substations. To alert all the powerhouses and substations and to have every trans-

4

former house watched would be a major job, and he could not justify giving instructions for it yet.

Yet.

Instinctively, Gideon believed that serious trouble was brewing.

He decided that in the morning he would send a teletype message out to all London police stations, telling them to be alert for any signs of trouble. But once he had made the decision, he had a feeling of disquiet; he should have done it today, not waited until tomorrow. It was difficult to arrange at night; it could be done through Information, but routine instructions should never be allowed to interfere with the rush hour of crime. Between seven o'clock and ten, the rate of crime would rise dramatically; most of the police stations would be stretched to the limit of their resources.

But first thing in the morning—

He tried to put the sabotage out of his mind as he drove along the Embankment, into Fulham, then along the New King's Road. There had been hardly any changes here since he had gone to live in Burlingham, the better residential part of Fulham; that was over twenty-five years ago. Now he passed through Eel Brook Common, then Parson's Green, well-tended parks in the heart of the colonies of small and medium-sized houses. Most of the houses were also well tended; only here and there was one in need of paint. London looked prosperous, but prosperous or not, think of what could happen to the tens of thousands who lived within a stone's throw of the local electrical power supply if serious trouble did develop.

He turned in to the street where he lived—Harrington Street—and saw his own house, solid as the Victorian age when it had been built, painted white and black against weathered red brick. He could see Kate, his wife, tending a window box of begonias; tall, slim-waisted, and full-bosomed, her hair a most attractive gray, she appeared to him to be

5

quite lovely. As he pulled up, she turned and her face brightened.

"George, you're early! That's wonderful!" Then she stopped moving toward him, and the watering can drooped in her hand. "Or do you have to go back to the office?"

"No, *Doctor Zhivago* for us!" Gideon reassured her. "That's if you can get ready in time."

A look of real understanding and affection passed between them.

"We'll be in time if you don't take too long over dinner," she said as they went into the house.

"Are we on our own?" Gideon asked.

"Yes—everybody's out tonight," Kate said, a little forlornly. But her mood passed quickly. Soon Gideon was eating lamb cutlets, French beans, and fried potatoes, and Kate was making herself an omelette in a kitchen which had been modern thirty years before, and was still in shining order.

As the Gideons drove from Fulham to Kensington, where *Doctor Zhivago* was having a third or fourth run, giving them a last chance to catch up with it, a small man in a coverall —not unlike the truck driver—was filling the oil cans at the Battersea Power Station.

He used the proper oil.

There were no incidents there, or anywhere else in power stations, substations, or transformers, that night.

The man who filled the oil cans finished his shift at ten o'clock and went home with all the other workers on the shift. He cycled from the yard of the power station to his home in a narrow street in Wandsworth, across the Thames from Fulham, put his bicycle in a garden shed, and went into the house by the back door.

A light showed from the passage, and he called out, "You home, Lizzie?"

A door opened and television voices sounded.

"Jack, I never heard you!" His wife—broad, fat, unexpectedly flat-chested—came hurrying. "It's all right, love, dinner's in the oven. Do you want it right away or will you wash first?"

"I'll wash," he said.

He looked very tired as he walked up the narrow stairs while his wife bustled about in the kitchen; he washed his hands and face, then went into the storeroom where he did his office work, for he was secretary to several Pools and betting clubs. In the storeroom, unexpected in such a small terrace house, was a telephone.

He dialed.

His wife, at the foot of the stairs, heard the *ting!* of the bell and the noise as he dialed, but could not hear what he said.

"I was watched tonight," he said to a man who answered his ring. "I don't think they were after me special—just watching anyone who went near the oil cans."

"That's what we would expect," the other man said. "Don't do anything else at all unless we tell you to. Understand? Don't do anything."

"I won't," promised the innocent-looking little man.

He felt almost sorry, for last night he had done enough damage to harm half a million people. It gave him an intense satisfaction, which he did not recognize as a sense of power.

About the same time, another, very different kind of man was standing by his wife's side, looking down at their only daughter. Sheila was seven, and when she was born her mother had been just seventeen and he, Frank Morrison, nineteen. Then he had been a junior draftsman at Hibild, Limited; and then Hibild had been a small civil-engineering company, with only six in the drawing office. Now, spreading out over London, Hibild had become a vast organization, and he was a senior draftsman, with excellent prospects.

He had Lillian, his wife, whom he loved. He had Sheila, his daughter, whom he adored. He owned his own house in an estate overlooking Camberwell Green on the south side of

the river, his own minicar, everything he could possibly want
—except more children.

Lillian simply did not conceive again.

In the beginning, she had appeared to be as worried about
this as he was, and they had visited gynecologists of varying
reputation and importance, and all had said the same thing:
it was through no fault of his. Lillian had resigned herself
fairly quickly to the improbability of having more children.
He knew she was happy, and in a way so was he.

But his was a precarious happiness. Looking down on
Sheila as he did now, fear gripped him. Her fair hair was
beautiful, her fair skin was without a blemish, and she had
upsweeping gold-colored eyelashes. In fact, she was Lillian
all over again. The feeling of fear was very strong in him at
this moment, a kind of premonition that his state of well-
being was too good to last.

"Let's go, in case we wake her," Lillian said.

She wasn't really afraid of waking the child; she wanted to
see tonight's "Love Story" on television. He had some draw-
ings to look over; Hibild was estimating for a big new factory
near the Great West Road, and each senior draftsman had
been asked to present ideas. If he could work up a good one,
he would be well rewarded. The problem was tricky, however; the company wanted easy access to the Great West
Road and also easy access to the railway line, yet the amount
of space available simply wasn't enough unless they built
higher than the Town Planning Commission would permit.

"There must *be* a way," he said to himself.

"Shut the door, dear, if you're going upstairs," Lillian said,
already watching the screen.

As he stood at the big sloping desk in his room, Frank
Morrison's uneasiness subsided, and he lost himself in con-
centration.

In a back room of an old Georgian house in Brixton,
another man lay restless on his bed. The house was dilapi-

dated, the room in need of complete redecoration, the few oddments of furniture littered with unwashed cups and saucers, plates and dishes, clothes, old newspapers and magazines.

There was one feature about the newspapers and magazines that might have struck an even deeper chill into the heart of Frank Morrison. For they were all about police investigations into the abduction and murder of children about Sheila's age.

The man on the bed, whose name was Luke Oliver, saw visions. Pretty faces. Pretty faces surrounded by fair hair, faces of girls with lovely blue eyes. He didn't *want* to see them, but he did. They were all smiling at him, beckoning him.

He was sweating all over.

Even when he heard the clatter and din of fire engines, he took no notice. Nothing concerned him but faces. Pretty girls' faces. Blue-eyed faces. Baby faces. Pretty, blue-eyed baby faces . . .

2 The Fire

Old Walter Garratt loved the smell of wood.

He had been a carpenter all his life, and his seventy-year-old hands bore plenty of scars to show how often chisels and saws and screwdrivers had slipped. Ten years ago, one had slipped too far, and he had lost the fingers of his right hand. A widower even then, he had come out of the hospital unable to do the work he loved, but the resinous smell of newly sawed wood still attracted him irresistibly. He went back to the furniture manufacturers in Bethnal Green, on the north side of the Thames and in one of the most concentrated industrial-*cum*-residential areas of London, and asked for a job as night watchman.

"All right, Walter," old Jeff Mickle had said. "If that's what you want, that you shall have, lad."

He was now in his tenth year as night watchman at Mickle & Stratton, manufacturers of Easiphit Furniture, a family business with two Mickles and one Stratton on the Board. Old Jeff Mickle was still the boss, but he left much of the day-to-day running of the firm to the younger generation.

It was an old building, three stories of soot-darkened brick. All the heavy machinery was on the ground floor. Lifts and hoists moved the prepared wood up to the first floor for shaping and preparing, and to the second for assembly, upholstery, and polishing. There were no plastics at this plant, although another Mickle & Stratton plant only a mile away made nothing but plastic furniture. Walter kept to a regular schedule. He visited the clocks on each floor, turning a key on each one to show that he had been there.

The ground floor, with much more sawdust and shavings than the others, attracted him most, but there was something in the polishing shop that he liked, too. He always took especial care on the top floor, for polish and varnish could soon catch fire, and some of the youngsters these days were careless with their cigarette ends. He would stand around and sniff, almost as if he wanted a fire to break out. He looked a little like a wire-haired terrier, with his square face and woolly-looking, yellowish-gray hair. He was lean, too, and sprightly.

On the night that Gideon had taken Kate to the cinema, Walter Garratt finished a cheese sandwich, washed it down with hot coffee, and, at the stroke of nine-thirty, began his next round. It should take him exactly fifteen minutes. He went, as usual, straight up to the polishing shop, punched the clock, stood and sniffed, and found nothing at all the matter. He went down one flight of wooden steps to the middle floor, walking between bays filled with bed panels, chair frames, tables, cupboards, wardrobes, chests of drawers—a great variety of furniture of the kind which would be seen in any modest home. On one side were items which had been rejected on inspection.

"These young devils—don't know what it is to be careful," he grumbled.

He started down the next flight of steps with nothing more in his mind than this brief criticism, reached the foot, and stared across the wide space to the spot where the big saws were. Those electrically driven circular saws could cut through twelve inches of solid oak in the time it would take a man to cut through a piece of paper with a pair of scissors.

Standing by the biggest machine, on the far side, was a youth, who appeared to be quite as startled as Walter.

After the first shock, Walter said in his grating voice, "Now, what are you up to, my lad?"

"No-nothing!" the youth stammered. "Nothing!"

"Just come to pass the time of night, have yer?" Walter moved across the room, trying to remember where he had seen this lad before. He was short and very thin, with a pale, round face, and eyes as dark as polished wood. "How did you get in?"

The youth didn't answer.

"Ah!" exclaimed Walter. "I remember you now. You're in the upholstery department. You work with Ted Smith." He drew within a few yards of the other. "What's your name, son? It slips my memory for the moment. Come on, don't stand there looking like an idiot. What's your name and what are you doing here?"

He took a step forward.

The boy suddenly turned and ran toward the emergency exit which was nearest to him, and as he ran he flung something over his shoulder. It struck the circular-saw bench and burst into flames—and on the instant flames shot through the air in all directions, even close to the boy's head and face. They touched the shavings, which flared up, knee high in a split second; and as the youth opened the door and caused a draft more shavings came alight, and all Walter Garratt could see was fire.

"Fire!" he gasped. "My God! Fire!" He staggered toward the small corner office, where he spent most of his time, but as he drew near a sheet of flame caught some kindling wood, stacked in a corner for sacking next day. It was resinous, and dry—and it seemed to set the whole floor alight.

"Telephone," gasped Walter. "Must—reach—telephone."

He could have turned and escaped by the main entrance, but all he could think of was the telephone in his office. Flames cut him off from it. "I must *telephone*," he gasped, but there wasn't a chance, and he turned around.

A cloud of smoke caught at his throat and he began to cough. The coughing and the smoke made his eyes sting and he could not see which way he was going.

He couldn't stop coughing.

He couldn't stop choking.

He stood helplessly swaying, with the flames licking at his trousers, at his jacket. At his hair.

Police Constable Jack Race, a man in his late twenties, of N.E. Division, saw a youth cycling out of the private road of the Mickle & Stratton factory without his lights on. Race could not be positive, but he thought the youth had come from the gate of the yard, where timber was stored in big, open sheds. He wondered what anyone could want there at this hour. Had there been a boy *and* a girl, he would have thought nothing of it. But one youth, in a hurry, was suspicious.

He used his walkie-talkie.

"Seen a youth on a bicycle coming from Mickle & Stratton, in Dove Lane," he reported. "I'm going to take a look." He tucked his little transmitter into his top pocket and reached the gate. It was unlocked, and it shouldn't be. He pushed it open, stepped through, and immediately saw the flames through a window. "My God!" he gasped, and rushed toward the door immediately opposite the gate.

He reached it, only to pause.

One shouldn't open a door on a fire; it could cause a blast which might make it ten times worse. Already his walkie-talkie was in his hand. Why couldn't he switch the bloody thing on? His finger quivered, and at last steadied. "Race here again," he announced clearly. "Fire at Mickle & Stratton— looks as if it has a big hold."

"Anyone inside?" the Station Controller asked.

"I—I'll look," said Race.

He peered through the window. Flames seemed to cover the whole of the far end of the ground floor. He saw huge piles of planed wood burning, saw the staircase ablaze, saw a hole in the ceiling; and all the time thought, There's a watchman; I know there's a watchman.

Then he saw the man on the floor, flames licking all about him.

"My God!" gasped Race. "My God!"

The door was within his reach; he *could* get inside and try to reach the old man. Everything in his mind told him he should try, but something held him back. As if mesmerized, he saw the gray head, covered with flames, then saw the man actually move, *crawl*, away from the stairs, only to stop as more flames reached him. It was too late to help; obviously it was far too late; one didn't have to be a hero, didn't have to kill oneself.

He backed away.

Gerald Stratton was thinking, With a little bit of luck, I might pull this off.

"This" was Loretta Conti, the dark-haired, sloe-eyed girl with whom he was dancing. He did not know her well, only that she had beautiful dark eyes and a lovely olive-colored complexion, and the kind of figure that made him dream of bed. She was an acquaintance of Tony and Dee Mickle, his smugly married partners, and when the evening had started he had thought her as unattainable as Cleopatra. They had dined at the Ecu de France and then come on here, to the Cordon Bleu Club, for dancing; and she danced with a light, practiced ease. After the first bottle of champagne, her body had relaxed, too; she did not seem anything like as aloof as she had earlier. His cheek was against hers, and he held her a little closer.

The small room was deliberately intimate. The three-piece band played from a dais in one corner, so crowded that the instrumentalists seemed hardly to have elbowroom. Three other couples were dancing. Delphi, the Greek shipowner, was with his elderly, white-haired wife. Sir Geoffrey Craven of Hibild, Limited, was with a striking-looking woman. Stratton regarded Craven with particular respect, for Mickle & Stratton supplied a lot of built-in furniture on contract to Hibild, and he knew that Craven wanted to buy a controlling interest in the smaller firm; so far, old Jeff wouldn't hear of it.

The time would come when he would sell, though.

There was also a man whom Stratton did not know but to whom the proprietor, Emile Brunner, had been most deferential; so presumably he was rich. He was dancing with a Scandinavian-type blonde quite beautiful in her cold, silvered way; she wore an off-the-shoulder gown which was like a sheath over her body. Gerald had noticed all these things while sitting out, and was aware of them now that he was dancing, although the closeness of Loretta's touch made everything else seem of lesser importance.

The problem was to judge the moment to suggest going to his flat before taking her home. The right timing was essential, and much would depend on whether the champagne had mellowed her as much as he believed. Finish this dance, then another drink, another dance, and—

"Excuse me, Mr. Stratton." There was a hand at his shoulder and a voice in his ear—unthinkable at the Cordon Bleu. He glanced around, still holding Loretta, to see Erikson, the secretary of the club.

"What is it?" Stratton demanded, trying to conceal his annoyance.

"There is an urgent message from Mr. Mickle, sir."

From Tony at *this* hour?

"It must be a joke," he said.

"No, sir. Mrs. Mickle herself is on the line."

Stratton thought, in a curiously deflated kind of way, Dee's doing her rescue act. He eased his hold on Loretta but took her hand. "I've been called to the telephone," he said. "I won't be a moment." He led her to their table, motioned to the champagne in a silver bucket by the wall, and said to the waiter, "Look after Miss Conti, won't you?" He squeezed her hand before turning toward the door leading to the offices and the cloakrooms. A girl with red hair held a telephone toward him. He almost snatched it.

"Tony, what the devil—"

15

"The Dove Lane factory's on fire," said Tony levelly. "I'm at Willerby's across the road. How long will you be?"

Stratton caught his breath.

"Give me fifteen minutes," he said.

"Of course I understand," said Loretta as he handed her into a taxi. "I ought to have an early night, anyhow. I do hope you don't find things too bad."

Gerald Stratton had never seen more people crowded together, or more fire-fighting vehicles in one place. They lined one side of Dove Lane, leaving just room for smaller vehicles and firemen to pass, and they were pouring great streams of water onto nearby buildings. By now, only a gentle spray was falling onto the factory, which he had left only a few hours before as packed full of partly finished furniture as it could be. A policeman came up to him as he tried to force his way through a barrier.

"I'm afraid you can't—"

"Don't be a bloody fool. I'm Gerald Stratton."

"It doesn't matter who—" the policeman began, then broke off and echoed: *"Stratton."*

"I *own* the place."

"I'm sorry, sir. Mr. Mickle's waiting for you at a builders' yard along the road. Follow me, sir." The policeman led the way past dozens of firemen wearing steel helmets, and over hoses which seemed to coil in all directions like tormented worms. Water was everywhere, sometimes making pools inches deep. Stratton's thin-soled patent-leather shoes were soon soaked, chilling his feet, but the heat from the fire was sharp on his face. He could hardly think beyond the need for following the policeman.

Then they turned in to Willerby's, a builders' yard with a small shed for an office. The shed was open, lights were on, and against them Tony Mickle's plump figure showed in clear silhouette.

16

Tony, who had obviously seen him coming, approached and said without preamble, "There's no sign of Walter Garratt. They're afraid he's inside."

Stratton thought, Who the hell's Garratt? There was fifty thousand pounds' worth of furniture in that place, and—it's all gone. The whole building's gone.

"How the hell did the fire start?" he demanded stridently. "How did it start, that's what I want to know." Then he remembered that Garratt was the night watchman. "And why didn't Garratt warn us? Why—"

He broke off, seeing and understanding the expression on his partner's face.

"I'm sorry," he muttered.

That's the last time I'll employ a drunken old fool, he thought. My God, this will ruin us. It will ruin us! But in a few moments his spirits lifted, and he almost said aloud, Now we'll have to sell out.

3 The Briefing

Gideon woke a little after seven o'clock the next morning. Kate was still asleep, and he didn't disturb her but got out of bed and pushed his feet into slippers. He looked enormous in rumpled blue-striped pajamas, gaping at the belly, but in a strange way he also looked impressive. He himself was not greatly impressed by his unshaven face with its big features and full lips, but he had a moment of satisfaction because his thick gray hair, which grew back from his forehead, hardly needed a comb. He shrugged himself into a dressing gown and went downstairs to put the kettle on, and as he opened the kitchen door he heard a gasp and a rattle of cups.

"Careful!" his son Malcolm cried.

Malcolm, at nineteen, was the last of his sons still at "school"—a technical college where, after much vacillation, he had decided to study for computer management. In feature not unlike Gideon, he was a slender youth—too slender, his mother thought, for a boy of his age.

He was carrying a tea tray.

"Don't say that's for me," said Gideon.

"It is, as a matter of fact. I heard you get up."

"Didn't think I made a sound," Gideon said. "What were you doing prowling about so early?"

"Listening to the radio news," said Malcolm. "Shall I pour out?"

"Please." Gideon sat on the arm of a big kitchen chair. "Anything worth hearing?"

"The increase ratio of national productivity went down one and a half per cent last quarter," stated Malcolm solemnly.

A few years ago, he would not have had the faintest idea what the increase ratio of national productivity was, but he had become a very earnest young man and, as he was going into industry, had convinced himself that—cricket and football reports apart—the only news worth hearing had to do with industry and commerce.

Gideon took his tea and sipped; Malcolm's tea was always stinging hot, and exactly as he liked it—a little too strong for most, but not for Gideon.

"That's a blow," he said, as solemnly as his son.

"Oh, Dad, *do* take some things I say seriously!"

"As a matter of fact," said Gideon mildly, "I was wholly serious."

Malcolm, who had very light gray eyes, looked at him suspiciously.

"Honest?"

"Yes."

"How come?"

"We've had more than our share of crime in industry lately," Gideon said. "I've been studying it." He smothered a laugh at the fact that here he was, justifying himself with his youngest child. "And even the Yard knows that exports matter!"

"They got another kick in the pants last night," Malcolm reported.

"The increase ratio business, you mean?"

"No. There was a big fire out at Bethnal Green. A furniture factory which was exporting half the furniture it made. Dad—" Malcolm leaned against the sink, and took up a stance as if he were going to deliver a lecture. "Why *do* they still use these old firetraps? Why don't they have new buildings?"

"Can't afford 'em, I suppose," said Gideon.

"Well, we *ought* to be able to!"

"Yes," Gideon agreed. "Yes." It passed through his mind that Malcolm was not only serious, he was worried, and in a way so was he, Gideon. It was a common mistake to forget that one's younger children grew up and could think independently and constructively. "Malcolm, I don't have much time to study the economy of industry, or—"

"That's just the trouble! People of your generation just let things drift!"

Gideon held out his cup for more tea, seeing in his son's face a certain embarrassment at this youthful outburst. He said gravely, "We've had a lot to cope with, Malcolm. Each generation has its problems."

"That's all very well," said Malcolm, handing him the cup back. "But this *was* a firetrap. Not only was the night watchman burned to death, but the whole building was gutted. It said only two walls were left standing. Production in these old buildings must be inefficient, anyway. I just don't understand it."

Gideon said sharply, "Burned to death, did you say?"

"Yes."

"Did they give any clue as to how the fire started?"

"It said the police were investigating the possibility of arson."

"No doubt we are," said Gideon. "And if it was arson, the man's death was murder." He stood up, unusually aggressive in manner. "Any other news?"

"Not to speak of," Malcolm replied uneasily.

"Any electricity cuts?" asked Gideon.

"They didn't mention any," said Malcolm, puzzled by that question.

If there were any more power failures, the reports would probably come later, Gideon decided as he went upstairs to shave and bathe. He could not get the thought of the fire out of his mind, or the thought of what Malcolm had said. While he was bathing, he heard Kate talking to one of the girls.

20

Priscilla and Penelope still lived at home, each having a room now that Tom and Matthew, their elder sons, were married, and Prudence, their eldest daughter, was not only married but a mother.

Kate had bacon, eggs, and fried bread ready for him when he got downstairs. She was full of the scope and brilliance of *Doctor Zhivago* and did not appear to notice that Gideon was preoccupied.

As he drove toward the Yard on a misty morning which promised heat, Gideon looked at the smoke rising out of the power station's great stacks, a slow-moving, billowing mass which seemed to be a source of energy in itself. It was rising straight upward this morning; there wasn't a breath of wind. A police launch loomed out of the mist, and soon afterward a lighter, low in the water, carrying timber.

For furniture? Gideon wondered.

Gideon's office was on the second floor, at the head of a tall flight of stone steps. It overlooked the river, and from his window he could see the London County Hall, Westminster Bridge, and, in the other direction, Waterloo Bridge and the Royal Festival Hall; this morning, all the outlines were softened by the haze.

He turned to his desk.

Hobbs, his Deputy Commander, was on holiday somewhere in Scotland, probably with relatives; Hobbs had always been reticent about himself and his family. Lemaitre, for years his chief assistant, was now at N.E. Division as Superintendent: this would probably be his last posting. Gideon was very conscious, these days, of the fact that he dealt mostly with men younger than himself at the Yard. There were exceptions, in Fingerprints and the Laboratory, but whenever he had his briefing sessions all but one of the men would be in the early or middle forties.

They would all be able officers, too, committed to police work and trained in a way which would have been unbelievable in the days when he was on the beat.

He looked at his file, prepared by his stand-in assistant, whom Hobbs was training. This was a Scotsman, McAlistair, with a noticeable but unaggressive accent; he was ginger-haired and freckled, with pale blue eyes. On top of a file marked "New Cases" was a note: "Mr. Lemaitre will call you at 9.30."

It was now nine-twenty-eight.

Gideon sat down and opened the top file. The first one, as he had half expected, concerned the fire at Bethnal Green, which was in Lemaitre's manor. Was this what Lemaitre was so anxious to talk about? Gideon, skimming through two reports, made a mental note to call the chief of the London Fire Brigade, and to instigate further inquiries about the dead man, the night watchman Walter Garratt. (The name rang a bell somewhere in the back of his mind.)

One of his telephones rang, and he picked up the receiver. "Yes, Lem?"

"Thought you weren't going to turn up," complained Lemaitre, who was the only man on the Force who had ever been overfamiliar with the Commander. "It was arson."

Gideon said heavily, "Oh, was it?"

"Homemade petrol bomb, apparently. The fire boys say there's no doubt, but I'd like an assessor out as soon as it can be done—if that's all right with you," added Lemaitre, with belated deference.

"Won't the company arrange that?"

"Mickle & Stratton, you mean. They'll fix it through their insurance people, yes, but I'd like one of our own consultants," said Lemaitre. "I'm not sure what's going on."

Gideon said, "In what way?"

"Old Jeff Mickle's as straight as a die, but he doesn't do much in the business these days. I wouldn't trust Gerald Stratton with a penny," said Lemaitre. "He lives high on the hog, likes expensive women, gambles, and has a West End flat. Young Mickle, the other active partner, seems all right

22

—got a nice little wife, too—and they live in Islington, pretty well on the factory doorstep. What can you do, George?"

"I'll have a word with Carmichael," promised Gideon.

"That's a good idea. Ta. And there's another thing," Lemaitre went on. "One of my chaps—"

"Police Constable Jack Race saw a cyclist," began Gideon.

"O.K., you've read my report," approved Lemaitre. "I've had *two* other reports from passing motorists that a cyclist was seen turning out of Dove Lane, but haven't got a real clue yet. The thing is it might be one of the employees."

"What makes you say that?"

"Obviously knew his way about," Lemaitre told him. "The front gate was unlocked, so he'd got hold of a key. If you ask me, it's an inside job."

Lemaitre always had a positive opinion; thirty-six years of service in the Force had not cured him of jumping to conclusions early in every inquiry.

"Did this man Race get a close look at him?" asked Gideon.

"I haven't talked to Race yet," admitted Lemaitre. "He's downstairs, waiting. George—" He broke off, and muttered, "Sorry."

"Go on," Gideon urged.

"When can you talk to Carmichael?"

"In an hour or so, for certain. What's your hurry?"

"I want to be after Gerald Stratton," said Lemaitre grimly. "I don't know why but I've got a funny feeling about him. And if there's no doubt it's arson—"

"You said there *was* no doubt."

"*You* have to be convinced," Lemaitre retorted gruffly.

Gideon concealed a chuckle.

"I'll get down to it soon, Lem, and I'll start a few inquiries about your man Stratton—you don't want to do it at your end, I gather."

"Ta, George, that would be great! Just what I want. No, he knows all my chaps, and I don't know that I've got any bright enough for Stratton—pretty average lot down here these days." Lemaitre's tone was immeasurably brighter. "I'll send details over. I just have a feeling."

"I know your hunches," said Gideon. "Lem—"

"Yes, sir!"

"Had any power cuts lately?"

"Eh?"

"Power—electricity cuts."

"Had one this morning, as a matter of fact," said Lemaitre. "Only lasted about ten minutes, but a hell of a nuisance. What made you ask?"

Gideon said with great solemnity, "I just have a feeling."

Lemaitre caught his breath—and then positively cackled with laughter.

Gideon rang off, and made notes of what he had promised to do, reflecting ruefully that he could not rely absolutely on his memory these days; at one time he would have kept all this in his head without a moment's hesitation. Then he looked through the other files, and pressed the bell for McAlistair, who came in through a communicating door with the neat speed of a jack-in-the-box.

"Good morning, sir."

"Morning," returned Gideon. "Who's waiting?"

"No one's actually waiting," McAlistair answered. "Superintendent Jones will come as soon as you send for him, but the others can wait—there's nothing new in, apart from Mr. Jones's report." When Gideon didn't answer, McAlistair went on a little uneasily, "I could get the others along pretty quickly, but I thought you'd want to concentrate on the fire and the power failures."

Gideon said gruffly, "Don't start thinking for me, McAlistair."

"No, sir." McAlistair's voice was crestfallen.

"What's on your mind about power failures?"

"We've had seven in the Metropolitan area in the past nine

days," answered McAlistair, "and I could tell—I felt pretty sure you were particularly concerned about the one at Battersea."

Gideon studied the alert, eager face for a few moments, not quite sure what was best to do. McAlistair was obviously bright and he was right, but nothing justified the sending away of senior officers when they had been waiting—and expecting—the usual morning briefing. McAlistair became even more subdued under the scrutiny.

In his most genial voice, Gideon said, "If you want to lose seniority, all you have to do is start making decisions for me. I want to see everyone on the list between now and twelve noon, without fail. Now! You're right about the power station business. I don't like it a bit. I want Mr. Piluski here in twenty minutes."

"Very good, sir."

Gideon nodded dismissal, and sat back for a moment in his big chair with its padded back and seat and its polished wooden arms. In a day or two he would know whether McAlistair would really make good. If he showed resentment at this little homily, in any form, the odds would be against him. Gideon guessed all would be well, and then corrected himself wryly; he hoped all would be. He leaned forward and opened the morning letter file—and sat staring at the one on top.

It was the buff-colored letter form that prisoners in Her Majesty's jails were allowed to send out. There were ten words on it, written in a bold, flowing hand.

> COMMANDER GIDEON [it said],
> I DID NOT KILL MY WIFE.
>   GEOFFREY ENTWHISTLE

4 Yesterday

Gideon picked the flimsy letter up and stepped with it to the window. He remembered this man vividly, could picture his bony face and angular body, the tropical pallor of his skin, his big greenish-gray eyes, and most of all his bitter resignation. From the moment of his arrest, and throughout his trial, he had repeated over and over again, "I did not kill my wife."

How long ago was it? Two years, or three? Two. Golightly, the Superintendent who had been in charge of the investigation, had recently retired and gone to live in Australia, partly on pension, partly on a legacy received by his wife. He had always been very sure that he had caught the right man. So had the Public Prosecutor. So had the jury. Consequently, Entwhistle was now serving a life sentence in Dartmoor. Why send such a man to Dartmoor, Gideon wondered. Whatever else, Entwhistle wasn't a habitual criminal.

The jury had found that after being away from his wife for three years in tropical Africa, he had come back and strangled her. The whole gamut of circumstantial evidence had been unearthed—overheard quarrels, incompatibility, Entwhistle seen leaving the house and returning later, his tardy report that he had found his wife murdered.

"Look for a lover," Gideon had told the officer in charge. They had found no lover and no evidence of one. Three children of the marriage, ranging from a boy of eleven to a girl of four, had been skillfully questioned about friends visiting their mother, and neighbors had been questioned much

26

more directly, but there had been no evidence of an *affaire*. Margaret Entwhistle had gone out one or two evenings a week, during part of the three years, leaving her mother or neighbors as baby-sitters, but she had gone to a theatre, or evening classes at the Central London Art School, or to the pictures. Piece after piece of circumstantial evidence had fitted into the pattern, and yet—and yet Gideon had felt a little needle of doubt as to Entwhistle's guilt.

Now and again since, he had felt the prick of that needle.

It was not an unfamiliar feeling. He had felt it about other cases, and, in at least two events, had proved his instinct wrong; in them, justice had undoubtedly been done. It was less instinct, Gideon himself sometimes argued with Kate, than a sense of accumulated doubt. Some trifling piece of the puzzle couldn't be found, and without it guilt could not be entirely proved.

This letter was Entwhistle's way of reopening the case. It might simply be a despairing final attempt to get a pardon, and it was interesting that the prison governor had allowed the letter through; that suggested sympathy. There was nothing Gideon could do, at least for the time being, for he had reviewed the case with utmost care both before and after the verdict.

He marked the letter "Entwhistle Case file" and put it in one of the trays on his desk. The other correspondence was mostly routine: from county police forces, asking for or giving information about suspects or unsolved cases, from the Divisions on nonurgent matters, from two European countries with belated information about a gold smuggler now in jail—how long it sometimes took for information to catch up! He pressed the bell, and McAlistair did his jack-in-the-box act again.

"Mr. Piluski coming?" asked Gideon.

"He's on his way from Battersea, sir, but traffic might make him late."

"All right. Send a girl in."

"Right, sir."

The "girl," who came from a stenographers' pool, was at least fifty-five, gray-haired, with a pleasant, if homely, face and big rimless spectacles. She sat near Gideon, with her surprisingly nice legs crossed, and took down his dictation at a speed which intrigued him. Deliberately, he went faster and faster, and she kept pace without the slightest fumbling.

When they finished, he asked, "Got it all?"

"Yes, Commander." There was a hint of a smile in her brown eyes.

"Good. Bring it in yourself when it's done, will you?"

"Yes, sir." She went out, using the passage door, and Gideon sat back. It was almost a record; he had been dictating for twenty minutes without a telephone call. Could it be McAlistair, zealously protecting him? If so, he would really have to deal heavily with the man.

His telephone rang, and he plucked it up.

"Gideon."

"Mr. Carmichael of the London Fire Brigade is calling you, sir."

"Put him through," said Gideon, and had a quick mental image of Lemaitre. He decided that this call must be the result of some pretty assiduous wire-pulling.

Carmichael's voice was quite unmistakable—cultured and brittle. He was the Chief Officer of the Brigade, a man of Gideon's age, and they had come to know each other well during a highly concentrated investigation into a series of fires, started, it had developed, by a psychopath with an obsession about slums. With many officials, Gideon was cautious, not sure that there was mutual understanding. He had no such doubts with Carmichael.

"Good morning."

"Good morning, George. I won't keep you long. Have you looked into that Bethnal Green fire yet?"

"Very superficially," Gideon said.

"Go into it more deeply, will you? I've a feeling it's one of a series, caused by the same man—or at least in the same way," Carmichael added hastily. "Reminds me of the trouble in 1961, when Bishop started dozens of fires before you caught him."

"Then I'll look into it right away," Gideon promised. "Remember Lemaitre?"

"I certainly do! He's your man in N.E. Division now, isn't he?"

"Yes. He's just asked for an assessor independent of the insurance company."

"Very astute of him," approved Carmichael. "Whom will you send?"

"You name him."

"Sir Humphrey Briggs," Carmichael said, without a moment's hesitation.

"Right," said Gideon, and then added as an afterthought, "I suppose he's in the country—didn't he go to that conference in San Francisco?"

"He's back," Carmichael answered promptly. "Like his number?"

Gideon noted the number down, telling himself that Carmichael had almost certainly been in touch with Briggs; everybody was being most solicitous this morning. The solicitousness was a trifle, compared with the apprehension the Chief Fire Officer obviously felt. There were always fires; there were always individual cases of arson; but organized and systematic arson with a motive was a different matter altogether.

Gideon put in the call to Sir Humphrey Briggs and, while he waited, looked through the files of cases still unsolved and on which he had been personally consulted, or wanted regular reports. There was the missing Epping Forest child, for one—the all too familiar story of a young girl child lured by an unknown man into a car, an agonizing wait for her return, then notification to the police after too many wasted hours. If children were clocked in, if parents reported them missing within an hour, say, after they were due home, a tremendous lot of heartache, over and above the lives and suffering of the children, might well be saved. Funny, he hadn't thought of that before. He made a penciled note, "Earlier alert," and skimmed the previous day's routine reports. There had been more extensive searching by the police, by the military, and by some neighbors. That was a new development which he didn't much like. If people were playing at being vigilantes, they must be gravely dissatisfied with the work of the police.

He pressed the bell for McAlistair, but the door remained closed. He waited a couple of minutes, glancing through reports on a bank robbery, a post office raid, and a fraud case which the Yard and the City Police were working on together. And he made a note to have young Gerald Stratton of Mickle & Stratton checked carefully. Then he pressed again. This time, McAlistair appeared, though a little less quickly than was usual.

"Superintendent Piluski is here, sir," he announced.

"Shut the door," Gideon said, and as it closed he tapped the missing-child file. "Did you read this report?"

"Yes, sir."

"And you didn't think it urgent?"

McAlistair hesitated, as if trying to recall details, and then answered, "No, sir. It seemed routine to me."

"Read it again and see why it isn't," Gideon said.

As he finished, his telephone rang and he answered with his usual briskness.

"Gideon."

"Sir Humphrey Briggs, sir."

"Oh, yes. . . . Hallo, Sir Humphrey, Gideon of the Yard here. . . . I wonder if you . . ." He explained at some length while McAlistair waited and Briggs gave an occasional grunt.

"I'll go over at once," Briggs promised at last. "Will you be there?"

"I'm afraid not," Gideon said with real regret. "But I'll get

30

in touch with you later in the day. . . . That's fine. . . . Goodbye." Gideon rang off and looked up at McAlistair, going on with hardly a pause, "Have Mr. Honiwell in to see me as early as you can."

"He's out at Epping, sir."

"I should expect him to be. Find out what time he can get here without interfering with what he's doing—it mustn't be later than five o'clock."

"Very good, sir." McAlistair was looking shaken, and he gripped the file tightly.

"Put someone on this at once," added Gideon, giving him the note about Gerald Stratton. "And send Mr. Piluski in."

"Right away, sir!"

"And McAlistair—did you see the point of urgency in the report?"

"I'm afraid not, sir."

"Neighbors forming a kind of unofficial force," said Gideon.

"Oh, I see, sir!" But Gideon, nodding dismissal, did not think he did see.

The door closed on McAlistair, with a slight hiss from the hydraulic fixture at the top, then opened again almost immediately for McAlistair, not in sight, to say, "Mr. Piluski, sir."

Piluski came in, soft-footed.

It was obvious at a glance that he was not English; something about the leathery appearance of his face, lined—more accurately, grooved—at the lips and the eyes, gave this away. He had a big, square chin—not unlike Geoffrey Entwhistle's, Gideon thought, but Entwhistle's face was more refined. Piluski's had a droll look. His lips, very thick, were shaped almost like a harp. His eyes, deep-set, were so dark at the lids and lashes that it might almost be due to eyeshade. He was half-Polish, half-English, and had spent most of his life in England but was trilingual, Polish and German being his other languages. He was also an engineer of some standing and had qualifications for a dozen different professions, but had joined the police in the early days of the war and stayed at the Yard by choice. He was as valuable for his knowledge of civil engineering as he was for his languages.

"Good morning, sir." His English was almost accent-free.

"Morning. Anything new at Battersea?"

"Nothing at all," answered Piluski.

"Any more power cuts?" Gideon wanted to know.

"There was one in the East End for fourteen minutes this morning," Piluski answered. That would be the one Lemaitre had mentioned. "An oil feeder line was damaged, sir."

Gideon asked sharply, "Sabotage?"

"It looks very much like it," said Piluski. "I haven't been over to the power station but had a word with the manager on the telephone. It was fire. Could have been wear and tear but there's not much to say that it was."

"How many does that make?" Gideon asked.

"Seven in the past nine days, sir."

"Duration?"

"The shortest was this morning's, fourteen minutes. The longest was at Tottenham and Edmonton—the second one—of forty-three minutes."

"Do much damage?" asked Gideon. He was watching Piluski very closely, assessing the man for the task he had in mind.

"Actual damage to equipment probably not more than fifty thousand pounds in total, but loss in production, apart from the loss of time due to delayed trains and the general inconvenience, must have been very heavy indeed, sir."

"Millions of pounds' worth?" asked Gideon.

"Impossible to state accurately, sir—but certainly a million pounds or more."

"I see," said Gideon. "What ideas do you have about it?"

Piluski hesitated, slid his hand into a side pocket, then took it out again. Gideon caught the movement and noticed for the first time that the fingers of Piluski's left hand were badly stained with nicotine.

"Smoke if you want to," he said, and pushed a heavy glass ashtray toward the other.

A cigarette case and lighter came out in a flash.

"Thank you, sir!" Piluski lit up. "If by ideas you mean do I know or suspect who's doing it—no, sir. I haven't the slightest indication. But that in itself *is* an indication of a kind, I would think."

"You mean seven cases of sabotage in power stations or substations and not a single clue to any of the saboteurs?"

"That's it, sir. If we'd caught a couple of them and were on the track of another one or two, it wouldn't be so disturbing, but each act has been carried out intelligently and without leaving a clue. Each must have been very carefully planned by skilled men who knew how to cover their traces. They could be organized by the same people."

"Yes," said Gideon, sitting back. His misgivings about the case increased, but there was a substantial compensating factor in Piluski's calm appraisal and analysis of the situation. He was clearly the man to take charge of this job, and one to discuss it with, not simply to direct. "It's beginning to look like it. There could be another series of crimes going on simultaneously, spread over the same period." He paused to give Piluski a chance to comment, but all the other did was to draw deeply at the cigarette. "Arson," he added.

Piluski's hand stopped halfway to his mouth.

"Two of the power cuts were caused by fires which looked like arson, too," he stated flatly.

"Any ideas?" Gideon asked.

"About what in particular, sir?"

"Why it's happening?"

"No," answered Piluski, hunching his shoulders so that his head seemed to disappear into his neck. "I need more facts to build on before I can start having ideas." Gideon had no doubt that he was being deliberately evasive, but made no comment.

"Have you any suggestions about how to cope, sir?" Piluski said.

Gideon considered at some length.

Since last night, when he had paused to see the billowing smoke at Battersea, he had thought a great deal about this affair. Now he knew what he wanted to do, and action fell into three categories: what Piluski could do; what he, Gideon, could do without recourse to a higher authority; and what would have to be discussed with the Assistant Commissioner and possibly with the Commissioner himself.

"Yes," he said. "Want to make notes?"

"Not unless you wish me to, sir."

"All right. I want you to go to each one of the power stations and substations concerned—finish the lot either to-day or tomorrow. Get the fullest reports from the management, the resident security people, and our Divisions. Check the reports for overlapping, and draw up a comprehensive report based on all the evidence. Handle it your own way, within these limits."

Piluski's brown eyes acquired an almost unnatural brilliance.

"Thank you very much," he said.

"If you've anything else on hand which needs immediate attention, get someone else to take it over—refer it to me, if necessary. Take whatever help you need today and tomorrow, but make sure I have the report tomorrow night."

"It will be ready, sir."

Gideon pushed his chair back. "Right. I shall put an alert out to all Divisions and have them send men to all power stations except the seven you're doing, to find out if there's been any incipient act which might have led to sabotage. We only learn about it when it becomes serious. I'll have a summary of their reports ready by tomorrow night, too." He stood up. "Keep in close touch with me."

"I will," said Piluski, also getting up. "Good morning, sir."

Gideon grunted, "Morning."

That was at eleven-thirty-five.

Between then and twelve noon on that lovely September day, when the sun had broken through the haze and London was already warm, a diversity of things happened, each of which would bring reports to Gideon's office within the next few days.

In her classroom at Camberwell, Sheila Morrison was watching her teacher closely and trying to understand simple arithmetic. Outside, birds were singing and a motor mower clattering. Only a mile or so away, Luke Oliver was drinking coffee out of a dirty cup and reading the previous Sunday's newspapers, all of which had pictures of the search going on at Epping Forest, of the missing child, and of her mother and father.

In his sunlit, modern office at Hibild, Limited, Frank Morrison was studying the plans he had sketched the night before, with a growing sense of excitement. He might have thought up the very idea that was needed for the new factory. If he had, it would mean a fortune; he would certainly be promoted, and would become one of Sir Geoffrey Craven's bright young men.

Lillian was tilting her hat at the most becoming angle before going to meet Sheila on her way from school. Meeting Sheila was a bother, and very time-taking. It wasn't that she minded; it was just that there must be some better way of making sure children were safe. It was a pity no other child from the block went to the same school.

She smiled into the bedroom mirror.

She looked *very* pretty.

Satisfied, she tidied the bedroom before going out to meet her daughter. One drawer in the dressing table stuck. The workmanship was shocking these days!

She closed her front door at almost the moment that Luke Oliver closed his bedroom door to go out.

The particular piece of furniture she complained about, with the trademark "Easiphit," had been built in the Mickle & Stratton factory which was now a mass of smoldering rubble.

The site of the factory on Dove Lane was opposite the builders' yard and a timber yard. Some of the adjacent buildings and a certain amount of the timber had been scorched, but there had been no serious damage except to Mickle & Stratton, which had stood on a site of its own, with room all around it for vehicles to move. In one direction was Bethnal Green High Street, in the other West Ham. Sir Humphrey Briggs was at the site, big, moon-faced, uncommunicative. So was Chief Superintendent Lemaitre, a Cockney sparrow of a man. And so were Tony Mickle and Gerald Stratton, who had just drawn up in Stratton's sky-blue Jaguar. All were watched by elderly pensioners drawn to the place by the excitement, as well as by some of the firm's employees, who were standing about disconsolately while steel-helmeted firemen and demolition workers examined the two remaining walls of the old factory. Three newspapermen and a photographer were also hovering.

"You know what this means, Ted," said one of the employees. "Out of work for months for those of us over fifty. Wouldn't I like to get my hands on the swine who did it!"

"*I'd* break his neck," said the other man, whose name was Edward Smith.

5 *The Scene of the Fire*

Chief Superintendent Lemaitre, "Lem" to the police of a dozen counties, sensed and understood the mood of many of the people who were standing by. He also knew that he was on the threshold of a major inquiry, and that it had fallen right into his lap. As Gideon's chief assistant, he had for many years been used to playing second fiddle, and more than once he had been saved by other officers at the Yard from making grave mistakes. In the past few months, however, a change had come over Lemaitre. He was aware of it, without any conscious effort.

Now that he was virtually his own boss, he had much more self-confidence.

Moreover, he was at home in the East End of London. Centuries ago, when the Huguenots had been driven out of France for their supposedly heretical beliefs, a family of Lemaitres had been among them, but generations of marriage had almost bred the French blood out. Chief Superintendent Lemaitre pronounced his name "Lemaiter," and under pressure would aggressively assert his claim to being a Londoner. He had a bony face, a round head over which thinning dark hair was flattened by perfumed pomade, alert but tired-looking eyes. His scraggy neck and agitated Adam's apple were emphasized by a collar too big for him, and a blue and white spotted bow tie.

He heard the comments of men like Edward Smith as he talked with Sir Humphrey Briggs, a very big, heavy man with a bowler hat which he wore like a halo above his moon-shaped face. Briggs had an enormous paunch, to which he seemed to have added several inches since Lemaitre had last seen him. But he moved over the charred and uneven rubble nimbly enough, and readily bent down to examine pieces of it, though he breathed loudly as he straightened up. The local Fire Officer was with him, and Lemaitre heard them talking of residual ash, traces of petrol, fragments of the plastic in which it had been stored.

At last, Briggs said, "I'll take that for analysis, but you can work on the assumption that it was arson, Superintendent."

"Glad to have advance knowledge," Lemaitre said. "Any signs of human remains?"

"Yes. The night watchman, presumably—you'll have to get what's left to the morgue for autopsy."

"Poor devil."

"Don't quote me yet," Briggs urged.

"No, I won't. Can I tell the directors?" Lemaitre nodded in the direction of Stratton and Mickle.

As he did so, an old but highly polished black Rolls-Royce appeared at the end of Dove Lane, and young Tony Mickle turned and hurried toward it. He was a little too plump and his gray suit fitted him too tightly, especially around the bottom, but he was very efficient. He had put up a notice telling all employees to report later in the day at the builders' shed, and had been most cooperative with the police.

"Please yourself," Briggs said, watching the Rolls-Royce as it slowed down. "Who's that just arrived?"

"Old Jeff Mickle—one of the original founders of the firm," answered Lemaitre.

They walked slowly across the rubble, watching the scene. A chauffeur jumped down from the car, and Tony Mickle leaned into the rear of it. At first, there was a delay which seemed very long. Then the back of a man appeared, almost completely filling the door. He was supported on one side by young Tony Mickle and on the other by the chauffeur.

"My God!" exclaimed Briggs. "He's fatter than I am!"

"Puts away more food than anyone I've ever seen," confided Lemaitre. "Decent old codger, though."

At last, the huge man was clear of the door. He stood by the side of the car, surveying the scene like a modern Nero, and quite suddenly Lemaitre said, "Must be hell for him. Over fifty years since he started this business."

Everyone, including the firemen and the onlookers, was watching old Jeff Mickle. The photographer was already taking pictures of him, the newspapermen gathering close.

"I'd like to hear this," said Briggs, and began to move nearer.

Lemaitre had difficulty in keeping up with him, but they both stopped in their tracks when Jeff Mickle threw back his big head and bellowed: "I want all my employees *here*—come on, get a move on, don't stand about. Harry! What's slowing you down? Charlie, put a sock in it. Ted! What's keeping you?" The harsh, gravelly voice sounded startlingly loud and everyone looked amused except Gerald Stratton, on whose face was an expression of disgust. Lemaitre, glancing about him, saw how the junior partner of Mickle & Stratton drew farther away. "Come on, then!" roared Jeff Mickle. He beckoned everyone in sight, his face red, his arms thick and stubby, like an old-time bookmaker or music-hall comedian.

"Mr. Mickle, I'm from the *Evening News*," a man said. "Have you—"

"What I've got to say everyone can hear! Come on, you lot —now, listen! Mickle & Stratton won't let a thing like this stop them. No, sir, not now or at any time. Nobody's going to drive us out of business. The minute I heard about the fire, I started looking round for new premises—*and* I've found them. I've taken over the warehouse in Dock Lane, the old oil warehouse. Circular saws will be put in this week; the cement foundation will start tomorrow. I want all the department managers there this afternoon at three o'clock so we can get a move on. All the suppliers will play ball; we'll be making Easiphit Furniture again by next Monday—and don't you forget it. And don't forget Easiphit Furniture fits every house and every pocket!" He glared at the newspapermen. "Put *that* down, boys. *And* don't forget to tell the world nobody and nothing's going to put us out of business."

Someone among the several dozen people gathered around began to clap. Someone else cheered. Suddenly they were roaring their approval, the firemen and the demolition workers joining in. Gradually the tone of the shouting changed, and it became a song. "For he's a jolly good fellow, for he's a jolly good fellow, for he's a jolly good fell-fell-oh! And so say all of us!"

Old Jeff was holding his hands above his head, boxer-fashion. His son was beaming as if he could not hold his delight. Gerald Stratton watched, his expression supercilious, even bored.

"That's done me a lot of good," Sir Humphrey Briggs declared. "That man's quite a character—pity he's one of a dying generation. See you again soon, Superintendent."

The assessor stumped off toward his own car.

Lemaitre moved away from the crowd; this was no moment to talk to Jeff Mickle. He saw P.C. Race on duty at the far end of Dove Lane, and went toward him. Race drew himself up. Lemaitre did not quite understand his own reaction to this officer, except that he knew he did not like him, did not really trust him. He had known him only as a uniformed figure for several months; this morning was the first time that he had really talked to the man. He was used to being watched covertly, to knowing that men were often self-conscious in his presence, as with any senior officer, but there was something more than that about Race.

"Hear the speech and the plaudits, Constable?"

"Yes, sir, every word."

"Do you know Mr. Mickle senior?"

"Only by sight, sir."

"Had a good look at everyone here, have you?"

"Yes, sir, I've kept my eyes open."

"Hope you have. Seen anyone like the youth you glimpsed?"

"No, sir."

"Had any brain waves about him?"

"No, sir. I wish I had."

"Sure you wouldn't recognize him again?" asked Lemaitre.

"It was very dark, sir."

"Yes. But not inside the factory."

"I couldn't see the flames until I was in the yard, sir, and I didn't see anyone inside."

"Did you have a close look?"

"Yes, sir—and I kept the station informed all the time."

"That's what your walkie-talkie is for," remarked Lemaitre. "Be a bloody poor copper if you didn't. In my young days, we were lucky if we had a bicycle so we could get to a telephone quickly. Tell me again exactly what you saw." He noticed others drawing near, but did not see any reason why they shouldn't hear what P.C. Race was saying.

Race seemed to swallow hard, as if he were nervous.

"Well, sir, as I told you . . ."

Race was sweating. He thought, He thinks I'm lying. Then he thought, He can't have any idea, can't possibly.

Aloud, he was saying, "I saw the fire and immediately radioed the station. I considered opening the door, but it seemed to me unwise, sir. A draft can make a fire worse. Then I looked in a window, and all I could see were flames. If—if I'd known the watchman was there—" He broke off, hating the gaze of people nearby.

"Well, what would you have done?" demanded Lemaitre.

"Tried the door, sir."

"Although it might have fanned the flames?"

"I would have had to try to help him, sir."

"Yes," said Lemaitre. "Yes. Absolutely sure you didn't see anyone else about except the boy who cycled off?"

"I didn't say he was a boy, sir. I said he was a youth."

"But you wouldn't recognize him again," Lemaitre persisted.

"No, sir!"

"So he might have been a boy."

"I suppose so, sir." Race was becoming both confused and resentful.

"Or an old or a middle-aged man," Lemaitre remarked, apparently more to himself than to Race. "Did you notice anything peculiar about old Mickle today—in anything he said, I mean?"

"I couldn't understand why he kept on saying no one was going to drive him out of business."

"No," said Lemaitre. "Nor could I." He nodded, and went on his way.

Race, staring across the scene of destruction, did not see the blackened mess. He was back at the window, seeing old Walter Garratt lying there, crawling away from the staircase, clothes alight, but crawling; so he must have been alive.

Gradually, the picture faded from Race's mind, but it left him feeling weak and heavyhearted. A sergeant came up and spoke to him, and suddenly he realized that he was being told to sign off duty and go home. He must look all in. He must pull himself together. No one knew what he had done, or failed to do, and no one could ever find out.

If only the man hadn't *moved.*

Race reached his bed-sitting-room just after two o'clock.

That was the moment Sheila Morrison, holding her mother's hand lightly, saw three other girls a few yards ahead, broke free, and ran toward them.

Luke Oliver was on the opposite side of the road.

He watched the child, and his heart beat until he was almost suffocated. She was beautiful. Like a sunbeam, running. The light made radiance of her golden hair, of her beautiful eyes. And she was all golden—pretty face and long bare arms and long legs, bare halfway up the thighs. All the girls wore that kind of dress, but there was none as exciting as that particular child.

"Sheila!" her mother was calling. "Sheila! Come back!"

Sheila stopped and pirouetted around, laughing. She ran back to her mother, arms widespread, and Lillian entered into the fun, spreading her arms in welcome, catching and swinging the child from the ground.

Luke Oliver felt as if his heart would burst, and for the first time he stopped and stared openly, although he knew that was a thing he should not do. This time, it didn't matter, for the picture was such a delight that half a dozen people paused to look, and an elderly woman exclaimed, "Oh, I wish I had a camera!"

Oliver passed her as she looked around for approbation. Another woman nearby said, "So do I." But in a few seconds the little incident was over, cyclists pedaled on, the women stopped looking at the mother and child, a milk-roundsman drove along on his electric float. Farther away, by the entrance to the school, a crowd of older children gathered around a sweet stall. From the big, old-fashioned school, built about the time that the Mickle & Stratton factory had been built, came the summons of a bell.

Sheila, walking sedately now, released her hand again at the iron gates.

"Goodbye, Mummy."

"Goodbye, darling, and wait for me or come home with someone you know, remember."

"Oh, yes, Mummy, I'll remember." Sheila caught up with her friends again, and went skipping off.

Lillian walked briskly toward the corner, a dozen or so other parents about her, some pushing prams, some with toddlers walking. In her own way, Lillian was as attractive as her daughter but Oliver, now on the other side of the road, hardly noticed her. He was still dazzled by the golden radiance of the child.

6 The Children

Some seven miles away from Camberwell but on the same side of London's river, another golden-haired child was going to school.

She did not look happy. There was no spring in her step, no radiance in her eyes. She had better features than Sheila Morrison, and it was possible that she would grow up to be more attractive, but now there was a faint, almost perpetual frown on her face as she walked along, staring downward. The other children, gamboling over the green meadows that led up to the school, passed her by. Only one of the women, a teacher, took any notice of her. She watched this child's slow but deliberate walk until she went into the building.

A mother came rushing by, child at her hand.

"Hurry up, Doris, or you'll be late."

"All right, Mummy!"

"Hurry, now!"

The child Doris began to run, with other latecomers. The woman who had brought her noticed the teacher's subdued, preoccupied expression, and said, half laughing, half gasping, "You look as if you'd lost a pound and found a sixpence, Mrs. Davis!"

"I haven't lost or found anything," the schoolmistress said. "Did you notice the Entwhistle child, Mrs. May?"

"Which one?"

"The youngest one—Carol."

"No, I can't say I did. I must get Doris to school earlier—

it's ridiculous to have to run every day." Mrs. May was getting her breath back. "You're worried about Carol Entwhistle, aren't you? As if you haven't enough worries on your hands."

Hannah Davis didn't respond.

"The other two Entwhistle children are all right," the woman asserted.

They were neighbors, on a new estate only five minutes' walk away, Hannah Davis small and dark and always soberlooking, Mrs. May big and floppy and lighthearted. Each had three children, roughly the same ages; each had moved to the estate about the same time; but little else tallied between them. Hannah Davis's husband had been severely injured in a road accident several years earlier, and had suffered injuries which had prevented him from taking up his former work again. He was now an elevator operator at a big store in Richmond, bringing home only half the money he had once earned as a capstan operator at an electrical factory nearby. Mrs. May's husband managed a supermarket, and was in line for promotion; he earned at least three times as much as his neighbor.

"I must go in to school," Hannah Davis said. "How well do you know the Entwhistles, Mrs. May?"

"Not so well as all that—they keep themselves to themselves," the mother declared. "But I don't see if the older ones can take it all right, why it should affect the younger one. After all, she hardly knew her father; he was away from home practically all her life."

"That's so, of course, but children in the same families *do* differ a lot, you know."

"Well, Clive's a jolly enough little fellow. If you ask me," Mrs. May went on, as if the other had not spoken, "there's something a bit queer about Carol. I don't think she's quite normal. Do you know I don't think I've ever seen her laugh?"

"That's what worries me," replied Hannah Davis.

"You can't take everyone's troubles on your shoulders, so

45

don't worry about it so much," advised Mrs. May. "Those children are lucky to be together. It's not everyone, relatives or not, who would take three children of a murderer and give them a good home. If you ask me, the Entwhistles are a family in a million."

"Oh, I'm not criticizing the Entwhistles," said Hannah quickly. "I expect they're as worried as—" She broke off.

"Go on, say it! As worried as *you* are. I don't understand you, Mrs. Davis, I really don't. How's your husband these days—I don't seem to have seen him for ages."

"He's fine," Hannah said. "I *must* go."

She hurried off, the last to go into the school.

In fact, she meant that her husband was as good as he would ever be. She sometimes wondered whether Mrs. May, or any other of her teacher friends or neighbors, was discerning enough to realize what a distressing life she was living. She had to wake Fred, half dress him, get his breakfast, get him into the invalid car, which he could manage himself. Then there were the children. Then there was the problem of doing her job at the school. Then again there was Fred, tired, disgruntled, often bad-tempered and at best dispirited, in the evening. He could *just* put himself to bed.

She was not thinking about herself today, however, but of the Entwhistle children. They lived on the estate with cousins of the Geoffrey Entwhistle who had murdered his wife. It had been a sensational trial, especially because of the three children: Clive, aged eleven at the time; Jennifer, aged seven; and Carol, four. When it had first been known that the children were to come to Richmond, it had been a nine days' wonder, some approving, some—for reasons which Hannah Davis could never understand—arguing that the children ought to be sent much farther away from the Lewisham home where the murder had been committed. Their aunt and uncle were in their forties, too—too old for such young children. Clive and Jennifer mixed well, but Carol was on her own.

Hannah went into her classroom, and the noise subsided.

Yes, she *was* worried about Carol, and she wondered whether she could do the slightest good by going to see the Entwhistles, who were virtually the foster parents. She did not want to be told to mind her own business, but someone ought to try to help that child.

Gideon was also thinking of a child: the one who was missing and for whom Epping Forest was being searched. Honiwell, the Yard Superintendent in charge of the investigation, had just telephoned.

"They've found a child's shoe, and it's probably the missing child's," he had said. "Unless it's vital for me to come, sir, I'd like to stay here until dark. Can't do much after dark."

"No. How about coming to my place for supper?" Gideon suggested. "We can talk about the situation then."

"Good idea, sir! I'd like to. About half past eight, say?"

"Do fine," said Gideon.

He was thinking that he ought to warn Kate about a supper guest. At the same time, he was wondering whether to approach Sir Reginald Scott-Marle, the Commissioner, direct about the sabotage. The Assistant Commissioner was at a conference in the Midlands, but he was also very sensitive about his authority, and approach to the Commissioner should be made through him. Gideon scowled. The A.C., a comparatively new man, was efficient, was even likable, but he did have a passion for the proper channels. It did not raise Gideon's spirits when he reflected that he, Gideon, could have had the job, which had been offered to him by Scott-Marle something over a year ago.

He put in the call for Kate, and asked the operator, "Is the Commissioner in, do you know?"

"He was half an hour ago, sir."

"Thanks," said Gideon. It was now half past two, and if Scott-Marle had been in at two o'clock then he had had one of his notoriously frugal meals in his office. There was a belief, which Gideon did not know whether or not to share, that such meals indicated the Commissioner had indigestion and was not in a good mood.

The telephone rang, and the girl said, "Mrs. Gideon, sir."

"Hallo, Kate," said Gideon. "Are you going to be in tonight?"

"Well, I wasn't," Kate said. "Not until half past ninish. I'm going to hear Penny's recital at the Town Hall, but if—"

"Can you leave something in the oven for me and Matt Honiwell?"

"Yes, of course, dear. I'll put a casserole in, and make a trifle. Is he—*oh*. It's about the Epping search, I suppose."

"Yes, love. He can't get away until after dark."

"He'll be tired out," said Kate, almost reproachfully. Then she brightened. "It won't matter if I'm not in until later, then?"

"Might be better," Gideon said. He hated driving Kate out of the living room in the evening, but she would not want to hear the details of this case. "I—" He broke off, when his other telephone bell rang, said "See you later," and rang off. Almost immediately this bell rang again; someone was trying to get him on the direct outside line, someone through the Yard's exchange. He lifted both receivers at once, said "Just a moment" into the direct one and "Gideon" into the other.

It was Honiwell, and there could be little doubt of the reason for this call.

"George," he said. "We've found her. I wondered if you'd like to come out yourself."

Heavily, Gideon said, "Dead?"

"Raped and strangled."

"Oh, God," groaned Gideon. "Who found her?"

"We did."

That was a good thing; if the volunteer force of searchers had succeeded, it could have led to a crop of such organizations, most of which would be unwilling to cooperate or take orders.

"No, I won't come out," Gideon decided. "Can you still make it tonight?"

"It would help if you'll send a car."

"I'll fix it," Gideon promised.

"Thanks. And George . . ."

"Yes?"

"I think we ought to put this out on every television and radio channel tonight. People must look after their children better."

"I know," said Gideon gruffly. "I know. I'll see to the television angle."

"Thanks," said Honiwell.

Gideon hesitated before speaking into the other telephone. He might have been keeping anyone waiting, from the Commissioner downward, but that did not seem to matter.

"Sorry to keep you," he said at last.

"That's all right." It was Sir Humphrey Briggs, speaking in a subdued voice. "I gather from what you were saying that the child's been found in Epping Forest."

"Yes," Gideon said. "Couldn't be much worse."

"Bloody lunatics," Briggs growled. "Only a madman would—" He stopped. "You don't want moralizing from me at the moment, that I know. The Bethnal Green fire was arson, started by the kind of plastic petrol bomb which can be made by anyone with a knowledge of elementary chemistry. You could have another arson problem on your hands."

"Thought as much," said Gideon gruffly. "Thanks. When can I expect your detailed report?"

"Can you wait forty-eight hours?"

"If I must."

"I'll improve on it if I can. You can quote me now, if it will help," Briggs said, and rang off.

Gideon leaned back in his chair, linking his arms behind his neck, trying to absorb everything that had come to him in the past hour or two. It had been as busy and ominous a day as he had known for a long time, and he needed time to think, to get his priorities right.

There wasn't enough time, that was the trouble; not enough time, not enough men, not enough skill, not enough anything. That being the condition, how could he do his job properly?

Slowly, his mood changed.

He allowed everything he had been told to filter through his mind until he was satisfied that he would forget none of it, and then made himself consider what he should do next.

"I'll see to it," he had promised Honiwell, but it might not be so easy as all that. This was an issue on which the Assistant Commissioner ought to be consulted, and he couldn't be. Gideon deliberated and then made up his mind, asked for Scott-Marle, and was told he was engaged. Gideon rang off, made his usual penciled notes, but more neatly than he would have for his own consumption.

1. TV and radio cooperation—Epping. Photos. Special message to parents.
2. Vigilantes—so-called.
3. Earlier notification to police by parents.
4. General matters, power failures/sabotage.
5. Arson.

That was about the lot.

His inside telephone rang, and since he expected it to be Scott-Marle, he was about to speak with that little extra precision which Scott-Marle somehow contrived to demand; instead it was Lemaitre, excitedly exclaiming, "George! I think we've got him."

Gideon bit on a sarcastic "Am I supposed to know who you've got?" and asked mildly, "Who?"

"The arsonist last night!"

"Have you, then," said Gideon, suddenly excited. "You mean you've charged him?"

"No, but I'm having him watched," answered Lemaitre. "He's an apprentice named Jensen, George Jensen, in the cabinetmakers shop at the factory—what *was* the factory— and he was out about the time the fire was started last night.

He turned up very late, saying he'd heard about the fire. His hair and eyebrows are singed."

"Why haven't you picked him up?" asked Gideon.

"I thought we might wait and find out if anyone gets in touch with him," Lemaitre answered. "One of our chaps knows the family and I've got a pretty good dossier on him. Can't find any reason yet why he should start the fire. No grievance, no history of arson—an eighteen-year-old kid with decent habits, comes from a good family, has pretty normal types as friends. Can't see a kid of his kind doing this of his own accord. Someone almost certainly put him up to it."

Gideon said, "Give him the rest of the day, but no more."

"But, dammit—"

"Lem, I've a big load on my plate," Gideon said. "Talk to him tonight. We can't play games when it's a question of murder."

After a pause, Lemaitre said with an explosive sigh, "I suppose you're right. There's one other thing, though. The old boy who runs the firm keeps talking about no one's going to put him out of business."

"Do you know what he means?" asked Gideon.

"Not yet, but I'll find out," Lemaitre said. "See you." He rang off abruptly, probably put out, and Gideon replaced his receiver quite sure that he was right in wanting to bring George Jensen in for questioning, yet understanding how Lemaitre felt and what he wanted to do.

There was a lull of perhaps a minute before his telephone rang again. This time it was Scott-Marle, who said in his most formal voice, "Yes, Commander. I will see you in my office at four o'clock."

At half past three, Sheila Morrison came out of the gates of the school near Camberwell Green and looked among the crowd of parents for her mother, but her mother wasn't there. She waited in the playground for ten minutes, at first impatient, then was beguiled into a game of hopscotch with several other girls. The waiting parents collected their charges and went off. No one noticed that Sheila was the only really young child who was still there. The older children were distracted by some boys on the farther side of the playground, and left her on her own.

Several people were in the street, and several cars passed.

Sheila looked about her, uncertainly at first, but an Airedale dog, loping toward her, attracted her attention. It was almost as tall as she, and she stood still and waited for it, hands outstretched; she loved dogs and was not at all afraid of them. This one, beautifully marked from rich brown to near black, glanced at her and let her fingers run along its coat, then went on its way. Sheila, happy, skipped toward the corner.

As she did so, a man got out of a small car.

"Hallo, Sheila!" he exclaimed, beaming. "I've come instead of Mummy today." When she looked startled, he went on, "I'm your Uncle Dick—don't you remember?"

Sheila let him take her hands.

"I *think* I remember," she said.

He put his hands to her waist and lifted her high, as her father often did to her delight; she loved the swish of air about her face and the way her hair went upward, as if carried on wings, when she stopped moving. He lowered her and held her tightly—just like Daddy.

"In you get," he said, and stood by the open door.

Five people noticed them. *Five.*

Lillian Morrison studied herself in the mirror, tipped the tiny flowered hat to one side, considered the effect again, then shifted the position an inch or two. No one was watching her. This was a new "serve yourself" milliner's, with the hats on stands on every inch of floor and wall space, hats of all colors, mostly gay, many flimsy. On one wall were cloth and felt and more conventional hats for the coming winter; but it was such a beautiful day, and Lillian was thrilled and sorely tempted.

She put the hat down and picked up another, but didn't like it so much. She placed the favorite one on her head again and stood back. Two older women came in, hot and tired, and one said, "There isn't a chair anywhere."

"We've no time to sit down, anyhow," said the other.

"Time," breathed Lillian. My goodness, she'd forgotten the *time!* She glanced at the gold watch on her wrist—it was twenty-five past three; she would be late for Sheila. She thrust the hat back on a stand and rushed out, the girl at the cash desk looking at her indifferently as she said, "I've got to collect my little girl from school!" Outside, the pavement was crowded, and there was no bus in sight. The school was only a short distance away, and she began to walk purposefully. *Everybody* got in her way. Old people strolling at random, a fluttering group of Pakistani women, a big dog straining at a leash—everything and everybody. She kept glancing over her shoulder toward the bus that never came. She thought resentfully that bus service was getting worse and worse; if she could have caught a bus, she would have been at the school by now.

She reached crossroads and traffic lights, and they turned red. She darted into the road and a lorry swung around the corner, making her stagger back. The stench of diesel exhaust nearly made her sick.

"Careful, dear," an old woman warned.

Lillian fumed.

But the road was clearer on the other side, and she could hurry. Soon she saw the school. Then she saw a little knot of mothers at a pedestrian crossing, with their children. Sheila would be waiting, she would be all right; the very last thing she, Lillian, had said to her was "Wait for me or go home with somebody you know."

The playground was empty when Lillian arrived.

There was not a child in sight.

Sheila was sitting back, happily, with Uncle Dick, sucking a lolly. She did not notice that the way they were going home was different from usual.

Lemaitre, a little disgruntled after the talk with Gideon, looked through the various reports, including a new and possibly significant one—that young George Jensen often went to the branch of a well-known turf accountant's, a betting shop, in Mill Lane. As far as the police knew, the betting shop was legally run but they shouldn't let minors bet. He was deliberating on whether to send a man to the shop when his telephone bell rang.

"Sergeant Rumbold reporting, sir. You asked to be told when Mr. Mickle senior was home. He's home now, with the junior partner, Gerald Stratton."

"Right," said Lemaitre, and his decision was made for him. He wanted to talk to old Jeff Mickle quickly; everything else could wait. He sent for his car, and was at Mickle's home in Bethnal Green within fifteen minutes. It was a square, red brick Victorian house, standing in a large, beautifully kept garden. The door was opened by a small, elderly woman, whom Lemaitre knew by sight as Mrs. Mickle.

"The police," she breathed. "Does that mean you've got some news about the fire? You'd better come in."

"No news yet," Lemaitre said as he stepped inside.

As the front door closed, there was a roar from farther along the passage of a voice he would never forget after that morning.

"I don't give a tinker's cuss what you say, you young fool. *I'm not selling.* You can sell out to me—*I'll* pay what Hibild offers. That's all in the partnership agreement; just let me see you try to break it. You're out, see? 'O-U-T' spells *out!*"

The little woman said cautiously, "You'd better come in here." She opened a door on the right, and Lemaitre stepped into a small room as another door opened. He caught a glimpse of young Stratton, pale-faced and angry. Stratton did

54

not see him, but stormed out, shutting the front door with a fierce snap. There was a rumbling sound from along the passage, then a bellow.

"Martha! I want my tea!"

"I'll bring it at once, dear," called the woman. "There's a policeman waiting to see you."

"I don't want to see any bloody coppers! They're not worth the uniforms the ratepayers buy for 'em!" Mickle appeared in the doorway as Lemaitre stepped into the passage. For a few moments they glared at each other, while Mrs. Mickle disappeared, presumably toward the kitchen.

"Better come in," Mickle conceded grudgingly. "And if you want to know what that was about, my flicking junior partner wants me to sell out to Hibild. There ought to be a way of stopping them—if the Monopolies Commission can't do it, you coppers ought to find a way. Anyhow, I've got him fixed. He's got to offer to sell out to me first. Hibild can't buy without my permission."

"Do you think Hibild knows anything about the fire?" asked Lemaitre bluntly.

The old man hitched himself into an ill-fitting white jacket and said gruffly, *"Someone* paid to have it done, if you ask me. Hibild's been trying to buy me out for months, and when they can't get all they want they find a way of getting it bit by bit. Don't you coppers even know that?"

"How much proof have you got?" demanded Lemaitre.

"Proof? I don't need proof; it sticks out like the nose on your face."

"Maybe it does," Lemaitre said, "but we poor flicking coppers have got to have proof, see."

"I'm coming, dear," Mrs. Mickle called out. "I'm coming."

7 *Top Level*

"Sit down, George," Sir Reginald Scott-Marle said as he shook hands, and immediately Gideon knew that someone had been in his office when he had telephoned so formally. He was looking as fit as Gideon had ever seen him, very brown from two weeks on the Scottish moors, handsome in his austere way, gray hair cut short, eyes bright against the tan. It was some two months since they had met, for the new Assistant Commissioner was proud of his part as liaison between the working detective force and the senior man at the Yard. "What is worrying you? These children?"

"That's one thing," Gideon said. He sat in a wooden armchair in an office of medium size, rather sparsely furnished but with photographs and printed police data on the walls. One wall was lined with books, and Gideon knew that it held an extensive library on criminal investigation, forensic medicines, everything to do with police work. "They've found the Lyall child, at Epping Forest. Honiwell just telephoned me," Gideon went on.

Scott-Marle's reaction was a tightening of his lips.

"I suppose it was inevitable," he said at last. When Gideon didn't respond, he asked more challengingly in his crisp voice, "Don't you think it is? There has always to be a proportion of this kind of accident. I don't see how we can avoid it."

Clearly, Scott-Marle had been giving it some thought.

"I suppose there has," Gideon conceded. "If you can call this an accident."

"In its way, surely it is. Few parents are deliberately care-less, but none can maintain their watchfulness every minute of every day." Scott-Marle paused, and when Gideon didn't respond at once he went on almost heartily, "Even our men slip up sometimes when keeping a suspect under surveillance."

"Yes," agreed Gideon. "And yes, I agree that parents are bound to slip up. I wasn't thinking of that angle so much as the time lag between the child disappearing and our being notified. It's always several hours, I've known it to be twenty-four. People keep telling themselves that the child is bound to turn up. They inquire among the neighbors, even search themselves—they seem almost frightened to call us. If we could cut down that time gap, we might save some of the children. And if we caught one or two of the men before they did any harm, it might discourage others."

Scott-Marle listened attentively.

"Honiwell wants us to get television and radio to put out special warnings," Gideon went on. "If we showed a photograph, asked for the usual information, and added this request for immediate notification of any missing child, it might do a useful job."

"I should certainly do it," Scott-Marle said.

"Thank you, sir." Gideon was pleased not only because the agreement had come so promptly but because Scott-Marle must have been convinced the moment he heard the proposal. Now that he had thought of it, it seemed the obvious thing to do. Why was it that simple and obvious ideas were so often the last to come to mind?

"What time do you need to speak to the television and radio people?" asked Scott-Marle.

"Any time in the next hour, sir—the main news broadcasts don't start until sixish. There's one other thing about the Epping inquiry, and I can't say I like it much."

Scott-Marle frowned, as if trying to guess what Gideon meant.

"Go on," he said.

"The organized assistance from neighbors and local people is something new. We found that about twenty men and women had covered part of the forest before we got to it. There's not only the obvious danger that an inexpert search might destroy valuable clues, but it's a direct challenge to our authority, and I wouldn't like it to grow. On the other hand, we don't want to discourage the man in the street from helping us."

"No, we certainly don't," agreed Scott-Marle. "Is this urgent?"

"Not yet, sir."

"Let me think about it, and you think about it, too." Scott-Marle actually laughed. Something had put him in a good mood today; Gideon could never remember him being so genial in his office. "As if you need telling to do that!"

"I'll see what Honiwell thinks of the situation tonight," Gideon said. "There are two other matters, sir."

"Yes?"

"We appear to have a systematic campaign of arson on our hands," Gideon told him, and went into some detail. "Now that a man's been killed, we've murder as well as the fire investigation on the go." He was tempted to add that Lemaitre thought he knew who had caused last night's fire, but something stopped him. "It could possibly be tied in with the power station sabotage."

Scott-Marle echoed sharply, "Sabotage?"

"Didn't you know, sir?"

"No, I—" Scott-Marle broke off abruptly, and then added, "I haven't caught up with all the reports since I came back from Scotland. I knew there had been two or three short power failures, but—are you sure it's sabotage?"

"Yes," answered Gideon flatly, and told him why.

When he had finished, Scott-Marle got up, opened a drawer in a metal filing cabinet, took out a folder, and came back to the desk. There was a noticeable change in him: the good mood had gone; he was his normal cold, aloof self. He ran through some papers in the file, closed it, and pushed it aside.

"Do you have any ideas about this, Commander?"

"I think it could become extremely serious, sir."

"In what way, precisely?"

"So far, the blackouts have mostly taken place during daylight hours," Gideon said. "If we have a big one after dark, it will give thieves a night out—especially if some of them have been alerted to expect an after-dark blackout. It's already dark by eight o'clock—a lot of places would be easy to raid." When Scott-Marle didn't reply, Gideon went on doggedly, "I don't say it *is* being laid on by a gang, but we've had at least four major crimes masterminded in the past eighteen months, and we've never caught up with the real leaders." He gave Scott-Marle another chance to comment, then went on uneasily, "Each crime has been very carefully and cunningly planned. Since the Great Train Robbery, we know we're liable to run up against a very different type of criminal from those of the past. Some clever and educated men now think ahead and pay in advance for information and assistance. I'd rather be well prepared for a major attempt than be caught napping."

He nearly added, "Again."

"No doubt you would," Scott-Marle said dryly. "What have you done and what do you want to do?"

At least he didn't suggest that Gideon was talking nonsense. Gideon told him what Piluski was doing and what he had instructed the Divisions to do, and added formally, "I'd like your authority to approach the Minister of Power, sir, as well as the largest industrial users in the area, and also the Confederation of British Industry."

Scott-Marle stared.

"It may be best for you to approach the Minister of Power through the Home Secretary, sir." Gideon should have put it that way round first, of course—Scott-Marle could also be very punctilious about the proper channels. What had affected him, and changed his manner so completely?

"What makes you feel that these moves are advisable?" he asked.

"It's simply a question of not being caught napping, sir."

"You intend to put in a request for an all-out cooperation in identifying the saboteurs, is that it?"

"More than that. If all power stations and substations are given instructions from the top, they'll be more likely to cooperate quickly. They all have their own security forces and are inclined to think they are fully competent to handle their own affairs."

"And you don't think they are?"

Gideon shifted in his chair.

"They're all right when dealing with their own internal problems," Gideon said, "but they haven't any way of working with other industries or other companies, whereas we have. But we can't—*I* can't—go to every individual firm and start from scratch. It would take too long even if they all cooperated, which they certainly would not do. On the other hand, if they had a recommendation from the CBI—or if nationalized industry had a direction from the Minister— then we would get cooperation."

"Yes," Scott-Marle said. "We might indeed." He stood up again, went to his window and looked out over the river, then turned and faced Gideon squarely. "What is your *real* concern, George?"

"George" again; that was better!

"We can't afford to lose production," Gideon said quietly. "Everything else I've said is valid, but—well, a quarter to a third of the total industry in Great Britain is centered in the Greater London area. A series of short blackouts like this can do more cumulative damage than one long one. Work stops, conveyors stop, furnaces go cold, men lose the working rhythm. I think it could become very serious on the industrial front, sir. That may be no business of mine, but catching the saboteurs is—and I'd like to have as much elbowroom as I can."

Scott-Marle took his chair again.

"I'll talk to the Home Secretary," he promised. "You prepare your schedule of operations. You can take it from me that you'll get the cooperation. One has only to threaten productivity losses and even the Ministries jump, these days. Decide exactly what kind of cooperation you think is necessary."

"I'll get started at once, sir." Gideon put his hands on the arms of his chair.

"Hobbs is away, isn't he?" asked Scott-Marle.

"Yes, sir."

"Want him back to help with this?"

"May I have twenty-four hours to think about that?"

"Yes. Mr. Guthrie isn't due back until tomorrow evening, is he?"

"No, sir." Guthrie was the Assistant Commissioner for Crime.

"Then come direct to me on anything which arises. I will brief him."

"Very good, sir." At last Gideon understood what had happened. Guthrie hadn't sent through a report on the sabotage, and Scott-Marle had checked in the file, to make sure. Now Scott-Marle was instructing him to go over Guthrie's head. Difficulties could arise from this, but he need not worry himself unduly; Guthrie wasn't half the man Scott-Marle was. On the whole, it could not have worked out better. Gideon stood up, not sure whether to say how much this mattered to him.

Scott-Marle stepped to the door with him, touched the handle, and said, "Did you know my daughter was expecting a child, George?"

Gideon caught his breath.

"I'd no idea, sir!"

"I heard only this afternoon that mother and child are

doing well," Scott-Marle told him. "I hadn't realized that one could get positively excited over a first grandchild."

"Hadn't you, sir? I could have told you!"

They looked at each other, eyes twinkling. In that moment, all thought of crime, all anxieties were forgotten. It was a good moment. Gideon, hardly aware that they were shaking hands, found himself saying, "Congratulations, sir."

"Thank you," said Scott-Marle. "Keep in close touch, George."

He opened the door, and Gideon went out. He walked quite slowly to his office, savoring that memorable moment until he reached the window, but this afternoon he was hardly conscious of the water or of the sunlight shining from behind the building and touching the whole of Westminster Bridge and the buildings on the other side of the river with grandeur.

Slowly he turned, then began to rough out the few sentences he wanted for the news broadcasts. It was a pity Hobbs wasn't here; he had a gift for the right phrase, and would do it in half the time. Finally, he was satisfied, and rang for McAlistair. At the same time, there was a tap at the passage door.

"Come in," he called.

Both doors opened simultaneously, and a sudden draft sent the paper flying into the face of the woman from the secretarial pool. For a split second, confusion and chaos reigned. Both the woman and McAlistair stood by their respective doors, staring at Gideon.

The woman suddenly bent down to pick up the piece of paper, and the file she was holding slipped; all the letters he had dictated fanned out in a neat pattern between her and Gideon.

Gideon said, "That's the message for the B.B.C. and I.T.A., McAlistair. Get it out on the teletype immediately and have Information make the usual approach to both authorities."

She held out the paper in her hand.

"This one?" she asked.

"Yes."

McAlistair took it, and seemed to fly out of the room. Gideon bent down in a gesture to help pick up the letters, and was quietly but unmistakably repulsed.

A telephone bell rang, and Gideon stepped across to it. Unflustered, the woman collected the letters and placed them neatly out on Gideon's desk. His caller was Lemaitre, but in that moment Gideon had neither time nor patience for Lemaitre.

"What is it? Unless it's urgent—"

"We can't find young Jensen," Lemaitre said in a hollow voice. "He's slipped our men."

"You bloody fool!" Gideon growled. "Send a description and all details out quick; let's put out a general call." He slammed down the receiver, in that moment furiously angry, and found himself looking into the calm eyes behind rimless spectacles.

"Shall I come back, Commander?"

"No," Gideon said gruffly. "I'll sign them and you put them in their envelopes. Let's make sure something goes right today."

Demurely, she drew up a chair.

There were seventeen letters. He read each one carefully, without needing to make a single alteration. He signed each with his big, bold signature, watching them being slipped into their envelopes. His temper had cooled and he was in a much calmer mood.

"I'd like you to come whenever I need help and you're free," Gideon said. "What's your name?"

"Sabrina Sale," she answered.

"Sab—" He checked a smile. " 'S-A-L-E'?"

"Yes, Commander."

"Thank you, Miss Sale."

"Thank *you*, Commander."

She went out and closed the door.

8 George Jensen

George Jensen paused by the front door of the house in Mill Lane, not far from Whitechapel Station, and stood for a moment in the hall. It was a tiny house, one of a terrace, and a small board outside announced: "SMITH & KANO, STOCK EXCHANGE BROKERS." Next door, two similar houses had been knocked into one, and a board announced: "JACKIE SPRATT'S BETTING SHOP."

Jensen went into the betting shop but, instead of going to the counter, slipped through a side door and into the broker's office. Inside it looked different. Outside it looked mean and badly kept; inside the walls and ceilings were freshly papered and the woodwork painted. A door on the right opened into a pleasant front room, furnished in much better style than most houses in the shabby street. In the next room, there was an office with several typewriters.

A man called, "Who's that?"

"It—it's George Jensen," the youth answered.

Almost at once, there was a scraping of chair legs and a man appeared in the office doorway. He was of medium height and lean, and wore a white shirt with long sleeves, and a bow tie and tight-fitting trousers. His dark hair and big horn-rimmed glasses made his face look very pale.

"What the hell are *you* doing here?"

Jensen said, "I—I had to see you."

"Why didn't you telephone?"

"I—I wasn't near a telephone. I came in from next door; no one—"

"There are telephones at every other corner," the man in shirt sleeves said harshly. "What's going on?"

Jensen didn't answer; he was quivering too much and couldn't find words.

The other drew nearer, and looked at him closely. Realizing that he was suffering from shock, he gripped George's shoulder firmly and took him into the office. There were three desks, two of them empty. In front of the fireplace stood an easy chair. He pushed Jensen into it, then took whisky and soda from a shelf, poured out a drink, and put it into the youth's hand.

"Drink up, then tell me all about it," he urged.

Jensen sipped slowly. His face was sticky with sweat, his collar damp, his eyes darted all over the place rather than look directly at the man, who stepped across and closed the door.

"Well, what's got under your skin?" he demanded more roughly.

"I—I've been followed," Jensen muttered.

"What do you mean, followed?"

"The—the cops—" Jensen began.

"The *police*," echoed the man in strident alarm. "Do you mean you've led the cops here? Why, you—" He sprang around to the door, opened it, and called, "Charlie!"

Almost immediately, another man called, "Want me?" There were footsteps on the stairs.

"Find out if we're being watched!"

"Right away."

"If we are, I want to know, quick."

"O.K., O.K.!" The man named Charlie went up the stairs again, not down; the other turned back in to the office.

"Now, tell me all about it," he ordered in a taut voice.

Jensen began nervously, but soon gathered confidence. He had done exactly what he had been told to do the previous night, he said, and he didn't think he had been seen, but since the middle of the morning he had been followed—and immediately after dinner he had been followed again by two men who he knew were from the local Division. They had not questioned him, but he had met a pal who had told him the police were asking a lot of questions about him.

At last, the story and the whisky were finished; George Jensen looked flushed, and almost bold.

"So I thought you ought to know," he stated. "That's why I came."

"I certainly had to know," agreed the man in the white shirt. "But in future you get word through by telephone—do you understand?"

"Yes, O.K., but—"

"There aren't any 'but's,' " the man growled.

A telephone on his desk rang, and he answered it with a swift cat-like movement. Charlie's voice sounded quite loud in the room; Jensen, as well as the man in shirt sleeves, could hear it.

"No one's about," he said. "We're not being watched."

"There you are, see!" cried Jensen. "It's O.K.! But—I've got to go into hiding, you can see that, can't you?" A cunning glint brightened his eyes. "The cops can't catch me if they don't know where I am, can they?"

"You never said a truer word," agreed the man in shirt sleeves. "I'll fix it soon. Want another drink?"

"Well, I wouldn't mind," said Jensen. He was thinking that he had done exactly the right thing by coming here. He had been afraid that this man might turn on him, but he need not have worried. That meant he was *very* useful to them. It was the third job he'd done, and there would be others—at fifty quid a time. Last night, after seeing the old man and afterward the copper, he had sworn that he would never do another; they could keep their money. It was very clever, really—he did the job, and then came here to collect his dough, his "winnings." He was very pleased with himself, and the second drink was just right. He was in the money, he was getting a taste for Scotch, everything was fine.

Suddenly, overwhelmingly, he felt tired.

He went to sleep ten minutes after finishing the second whisky.

He was dead half an hour afterward. His body was loaded into a canvas sack and taken by van to a small chemical plant nearby. Among the acids manufactured at the plant was sulfuric acid, for industrial purposes, and there was a large vat of concentrated sulfuric acid between the second and third floors. There were also a number of plastic containers—tiny Molotov cocktails.

Only one man was on duty, and he opened the hatch of the vat and watched phlegmatically while the sack was lowered into the acid, on ropes which were eaten away in a few seconds. For all the emotion shown by anyone present, it might have been a sack of old clothes.

It was sheer chance that P.C. Race, out of uniform and off duty, passed along Mill Lane five minutes afterward. He was within inches of the bicycle he had seen on the night of the fire, without dreaming of it.

At that very moment, Frank Morrison opened the door of his pleasant home.

He was puzzled because Sheila usually came running, and Lillian always made a point of being here unless she had warned him in advance that they would be out. In spite of the warm evening, the front door and all the windows were closed—they *were* out, then.

He walked around to the back garden.

The swing hung idly from the iron stand which he had bought for Sheila's last birthday. Her tricycle was on its side —how any child could always leave a three-wheeled bicycle off its wheels was beyond his understanding. He straightened it absently, more amused than vexed. A heap of wooden building bricks stood by a little sandpit which was filled with rubber and plastic toys. Everything was normal, except the silence. Children were playing in a garden not far off, but he could not see them.

He let himself in by the back door, which wasn't locked, and this was even more puzzling, for Lillian was very careful about leaving the house locked up whenever she was out. He did not understand it, but perhaps it was partly his fault; he was very prompt tonight—in fact, more than five minutes early. In a few minutes he would hear Sheila, then see her running in that gazelle-like way of hers, for him to catch and hold high, tossing her up and down several times before putting her gently on her feet.

He heard a knock at the front door.

Had Lillian forgotten her key?

He went to open the door, and saw a policeman standing there. He was so surprised that he backed a pace before saying, "Good—good afternoon."

"Good evening, sir. Are you Mr. Morrison?"

"Yes, I—" Morrison broke off, suddenly appalled, awfully aware that this visit must have something to do with Sheila and Lillian. Not an accident, please God, not an accident! "What is it, Officer?" he made himself ask.

"It's probably nothing to worry about, sir," said the policeman, and for the first time Frank noticed that he was a sergeant. "Your wife is down at the station, helping us with our inquiries."

Frank stared, almost stupidly.

"Inquiries about what?"

"Your little girl didn't arrive home from school," the sergeant said. "Your wife advised us as soon as she realized the child was late, and we hope to find her very soon. Would you like to come down to the station, sir? Your wife is rather—rather worked up."

Morrison said in a strange voice, "Are you telling me that my daughter has been—abducted?"

"It's much more likely she's wandering round the shops,

sir, or with friends. We've taken it very seriously just in case, but—"

"My wife was supposed to meet her at school."

"So we understand, sir, but she was delayed. If you would care to come along with me . . ."

Then Morrison saw a car standing at the curb.

He did not speak and he did not move, just stood there. He began to feel coldness creep upon him: first his chest, then his hands, then his arms and legs. It was like a chill which had taken hold of his heart and was spreading throughout his body. He could not move or speak. He could only stare at the big, middle-aged man in front of him.

"I'm sure your wife needs you, sir," the police sergeant said.

Morrison still didn't speak or move.

He could picture Sheila in his mind's eye: only Sheila. He could imagine her running along that path but could see nothing beyond her. Just her long golden-tanned legs and waving golden-tanned arms, the spun gold of her hair, and the radiance of her face.

He felt his head going round and round.

"Now, take it easy, sir." The sergeant touched his shoulder to steady him. "It'll almost certainly be all right. If you'll come along to the station—"

Morrison suddenly moved and flung off the helping hand.

"I want my daughter! Understand? I want my daughter! Every policeman in London's got to look for my daughter." His voice was pitched on a high key, but he did not shout. *I want my daughter.*"

"You can be absolutely sure that everything possible will be done, sir. If you'll pardon me saying so, your wife needs you. She's very upset. Would you care to have a drink to steady your nerves?"

"I don't drink," Morrison said. "My nerves are all right. *I want my daughter.*"

"I quite understand, sir." There was a pause, and then the

69

sergeant asked awkwardly, "Would you like us to fetch your wife?"

"I want to know what is being done to find my daughter."

"Everything possible, sir. If you'll come along to the station—"

In the Superintendent's office at the Richmond station, the sergeant spoke to his senior officer in a rueful voice.

"If you ask me, sir, I think it's knocked him off his rocker. He doesn't seem normal to me. He's with his wife now, but as cold as ice—seems to blame her for everything. All he keeps asking is what we're doing to find his daughter."

"Then let's tell him," the Superintendent said. "I'll come with you."

He went through as the sergeant opened the door, and as he went down the stairs he heard a woman sobbing. In the waiting room, the door of which was open, were three women —one of them in acute distress, her face cupped in her hands, her shoulders heaving—and one man. The man was smaller than average, with regular but unnoticeable features. His eyes looked like glass.

He strode toward the Superintendent.

"Are you in charge here? I want to know what you're doing to find my daughter."

"If you'll come this way, I'll show you," the Superintendent said quietly. "We have turned one of our offices into a special operations room, and you can be assured that every possible step is being taken." He led the way across the hall of the old building and pushed a big, heavy door open wide. Inside was a long, bench-like table with three men at telephones, a small radio transmitter, and a panel with a dozen different lights on it—a teletyper, at which a woman officer sat. "We notified Scotland Yard the moment we heard," went on the Superintendent. "They are sending extra staff, and additional extra staff is being drafted in from neighboring stations. A special call has gone out describing the car and the man who drove off with your daughter, and—"

He broke off, appalled by the change in Morrison's expression, the fury which blazed in his eyes, the way his whole body seemed to shake with rage.

"So she *was* kidnaped. She *was!*"

"She was certainly seen to go off with a man, sir, but—"

Morrison swung around. He caught everyone who was behind him by surprise, strode across the hall toward the room where his wife was sitting. Tears were streaming down her face, but she went utterly still when she saw her husband.

She didn't speak, but shrank away from him.

The Superintendent, one of Gideon's contemporaries, stretched his hands out toward Morrison, ready to grab him by the shoulders, for in that moment he looked capable of hitting his wife. But he did not. He stood and stared at her, and what looked like hatred twisted his lips.

"They'd better find her," he said. "They'd better find her."

9 Pressure

Gideon picked up the telephone without thinking; he was preoccupied with what he should prepare for the Ministry of Power and for the big industrial interests. He needed a more comprehensive picture of London's power stations and major plants. He knew many of them, but one of the depressing things about starting a new investigation was the discovery of how little one actually knew about those things one took for granted. He finished penciling a note on his pad: "Is there a map of Industrial London giving the powerhouses?" as the telephone bell rang.

"Gideon."

"Mr. Moore, sir, of Richmond."

"Put him through. . . . Hallo, Joe, how are you today?"

"Commander," said Joe Moore. "About this other missing child."

Gideon thought, What child? Then he realized what this might mean, and said, almost like a prayer, "Oh, dear God!" There was a long silence before he went on: "I didn't know. When did it happen?"

"An hour and a half ago. I've been trying to get you."

"Who did you get?"

"McAlistair."

Why hadn't McAlistair reported to him—or at least put a message on his desk?

"What's been done?" Gideon demanded.

"McAlistair didn't lose a minute," said Moore. "We've got

most of the help we need already, except enough to cordon off Wimbledon Common. How soon can we get the Army out for that?"

Gideon asked, "Do they know we may want them?" Why hadn't he been told?

"They're only waiting for confirmation from you."

Gideon picked up his other telephone.

"What command have you talked to?"

"Hounslow—a Colonel Dupont."

"I know Dupont," Gideon said, and as the operator answered he went on, "Get me Colonel Dupont of Hounslow Barracks." Into the other telephone, he added, "Got any description of the man?"

"Yes, better than average, too. It's already gone out. And the car was a black Hillman Minx, the latest model. The first numbers are 23 and a Y or K after that."

"That's something. I—" There was a voice in his other ear, a woman saying, "Colonel Dupont's on the line, sir." Thank heaven someone could be quick. "Colonel," Gideon said, "I'll be very glad of your help at Richmond."

"I've two companies ready and waiting," replied Colonel Dupont crisply. "The usual drill, I imagine."

"Yes."

"Glad to help," said Dupont. "Let me have it in writing, won't you?"

Gideon felt something like a laugh build up inside him, but it died almost immediately. Dupont did not even wait for an assurance, but rang off. The "usual drill" was that the troops would report at once to the Superintendent in charge of the investigation. He could go himself, but that could cause a delay, and even ten minutes might make the difference between the child's life and death. He turned to the other telephone, and heard Moore calling orders to someone. It sounded like "Then take her home. . . . What? . . . Can't stop him, can we?" There was a fractional pause, and then Moore spoke to Gideon. "You there, Commander?"

73

"Yes. Two companies are on their way."

"I've got Long at the Putney Heath approach; he knows what to do to cordon the Common off," Moore reported. "He'll brief the Army. Will you come over yourself?"

For the second time that day, Gideon said with reluctance, "No. You look after it. If you want any help—"

"Could Honiwell come over?" Moore asked.

"Yes," Gideon said, and wondered why he had not thought of that before. Honiwell was not only the Yard's expert on this kind of problem but he was familiar with the hundreds of "descriptions" of the man who had kidnaped the girl in Epping Forest. "I'll call him at once. Any other problems out there?"

"Not really," answered Moore. "The father of the missing girl insists on coming and helping with the search. I wish he wouldn't, but he seems so keyed up I think I'd better let him. It's a bad business," he added almost conversationally. "It was the wife's fault, in a way. One good thing—she didn't lose much time letting us know."

Gideon grunted, "That's something."

He rang off and sat back. The pressure of work, all the greater because Hobbs was on holiday, was beginning to weigh on him. He thought of McAlistair failing to inform him of the girl's disappearance, and came close to anger again. McAlistair had been getting under his skin all day, but this —this was unbelievable. Was the man hopelessly incompetent? The question was almost as unreasonable as McAlistair's behavior, Gideon told himself, and he must cool down before he sent for him.

He must ring Honiwell, too.

He ought to ring Lemaitre about the missing suspect.

He ought to find out how Piluski was doing.

He ought to be able to leave some of these things to McAlistair.

He ought to get a move on, and not sit back recapping like this.

He rang the bell for McAlistair, lifted a telephone and asked the operator to get Honiwell, then said stonily to McAlistair, "I'd like some tea." He put down the receiver, and the bell rang almost immediately. This time he hesitated before answering; it was no use showing his agitation with everyone who called.

"Yes?" he said.

"It's Lem here," said Lemaitre in a subdued voice which told Gideon that he had no good news. "No luck yet, I'm afraid."

Gideon thought bitterly, Why didn't I make him bring the boy in at once?

"Any trace at all?"

"Not really," said Lemaitre. "We've found out that young Jensen's been putting money on the gee-gees lately; that's something his parents didn't know. He's been going to a betting shop in Mill Lane, Whitechapel—Jackie Spratt's. It's some distance from where he lives and works, so that suggests he didn't want anyone to know what he was doing."

Why has he called to tell me this? Gideon wondered. Aloud, he said, "Well?"

"He was seen in the Whitechapel Road," said Lemaitre, "but as far as we can trace he didn't go to Spratt's this afternoon. On the other hand, I've been wondering about that particular Spratt's branch for a long time, and this is a chance to go and have a look round."

"Then why don't you?"

"Because I can't bloody well make up my mind, that's why!" Lemaitre exploded. "If he did go there and we haven't any proof, they can lie their way out of it. If he didn't, we've got under their skin—and Jackie Spratt's the biggest bookie in the East End. They've got shops and agents all over the place, and—"

"I know about Jackie's," Gideon said. "Try to find out whether young Jensen did go there this afternoon, before you question the staff in Mill Lane."

"O.K., I'll do that," said Lemaitre. "George—there's another thing."

"What is it?"

"I saw old Mickle, of Mickle & Stratton, today. He's convinced that Hibild was behind the fire. They've been trying to buy him out for a long time. His junior partner wanted to sell but Mickle's buying all his shares. Kicking him out, in effect."

Gideon, patient until then, demanded, "Come to the point, Lem."

"There isn't any point," said Lemaitre. "Except, Sir Geoffrey Craven's the chairman of the Board at Hibild."

"Well?"

"*And* he's on the Board of Jackie Spratt's, Limited," stated Lemaitre. "Thought it worth noting, George."

"It is and I've noted it," Gideon said. "Keep at it."

He put down the receiver and stared at the window. There was much more cloud about, and it looked like rain. The fine spell had broken as surely as the Yard's quiet spell. He now knew the real cause of Lemaitre's latest uneasiness, and it was not wholly because of the missing youth. Jackie Spratt's had betting accounts with practically every habitual criminal in the East End; they had a widespread organization, and had to be treated with respect, for they could make the life of the policeman on the beat unbearable. And they could give Division a lot of headaches, too, by arranging calls which needed immediate attention but would be mostly false alarms. Gideon was not even remotely in the mood to tackle Jackie Spratt's at this juncture, and Lemaitre no doubt realized it, but the possible involvement of Sir Geoffrey Craven was well worth noting.

The call from Honiwell came through, and Gideon pushed the East End problem out of his mind.

"Get over to Richmond and see Joe Moore, will you?" Gideon asked. "They've got a good description of the man who did this afternoon's job."

"I've been told, and it doesn't sound like the man I'm after," Honiwell said. "But I'll go right away. Don't wait for me tonight, will you?"

"Come up to my place from Richmond whatever time it is," Gideon said. "It's much nearer than Epping."

"Right, then, I will."

Honiwell rang off, and Gideon pulled some paper toward him and started halfheartedly to prepare the kind of questions needed for the industrialists and the Minister of Power. He had only just started when there was a tap at the door from McAlistair's room, and the door opened. McAlistair came in, carrying a tray with tea, sandwiches, and two cream cakes. Gideon watched as he put the tray down on a corner of the desk, forbore to ask why it hadn't been brought by messenger, but looked straight at the other man.

"Anything else, sir?" McAlistair asked with nervous brightness.

"Why didn't you inform me about the Richmond kidnaping?" Gideon demanded coldly.

McAlistair said, gasping, "But I did!"

Gideon felt his temper rising again, wondered what Hobbs could possibly see in this man, and wondered why he himself had never seen McAlistair's weaknesses before. In an even colder voice, he said, "I knew nothing about it."

"But I left a report, sir! You were with the Commissioner, and as Mr. Moore had the case well in hand I decided not to interrupt you. But there was a message on top of your file —I put it there myself."

He *couldn't* be lying.

Gideon said heavily, "It wasn't there when I came in."

"But I put—" McAlistair began, and then he changed the direction of his gaze, looking beneath the desk. "I think—I think it's on the floor, sir."

"On the floor?" exclaimed Gideon. "Why in God's name—"

McAlistair bent down, there was a rustle of paper, and then

he straightened up, much of his nervousness gone. He placed the sheet of paper in front of Gideon, and a red "URGENT," written across the top left-hand corner, could not fail to catch the eye. It was a simple, four-sentence report, containing all the relevant information.

"It must have blown—" began McAlistair.

"When the two doors opened," Gideon said. "Yes." He gave an unamused laugh. "Not your lucky day, is it?"

"I've known better," McAlistair admitted ruefully. "I'm sorry, sir. I didn't understand why you made no reference to the message, and just assumed you were satisfied with what had been done."

Gideon's telephone to the Yard exchange rang, and he was glad of the interruption. He picked up the receiver, and a man spoke immediately, tensely.

"I think we've got this afternoon's kidnaper, Commander!"

"Joe! How about the girl?"

"I'm afraid—" Moore began, and then someone shouted, and he said, "I'll call you back, sir," and rang off.

Luke Oliver crouched among the bushes, hearing the baying of dogs, the rustling of men moving slowly through the thick undergrowth, and, incongruously, birds singing and wasps and bees buzzing. The police seemed to be everywhere. He was disheveled from creeping away from the spot where he had lain with the child.

He remembered hazily everything that had happened, all that he had done to her. He was tired; he always was after he had passed through a period of such tension. He wanted to sleep. Had he had his way, he would have slept with the pretty child close to him; a doll-like child now, with her eyes closed. He had left her when he heard the dogs. Now, he knew, they were closing in on him and he did not think he would get away. They—they mustn't hurt him, that was the main thing. They must be merciful. He wasn't well; they must know he wasn't well. He was a sick man.

He heard a dog close by, and then saw a man's boots. The dog came nearer, growling, and he screamed, "Don't hurt me, don't hurt me!"

Someone nearby called, "We've got him, sir!"

Frank Morrison heard the words "We've got him, sir."

He was standing perhaps a hundred yards away from where the cry had come, by the side of his daughter. She was on a stretcher which was much too big for her, raised now onto a station wagon. A doctor was touching her wrist, but the examination was mere routine; he knew that she was dead.

"We've got him, sir!" came again.

Superintendent Moore and two other senior detectives moved toward the spot. A man in khaki uniform appeared from behind a patch of scrub, and waved. Another, with a dog straining at a leash, appeared from the other side of the bushes—and another man, in torn clothes and with scratches on his face, appeared between them. He had his hands above his head and he was calling out something which sounded like "Don't hurt me!"

The doctor, elderly, graying, said, "Come away, Morrison. We will do everything that can be done."

Morrison looked at him but didn't speak.

A woman, not far off, cried out, "Hanging's too good for him!"

Policemen and soldiers were gathering now, near the spot where the prisoner stood. Moore spoke to him but his voice did not travel.

"Come away," the doctor repeated.

Morrison moved, but toward, not away from, the prisoner. Two policemen were watching him, undoubtedly aware that in his present mood he might fling himself bodily at the prisoner in an attempt to kill him. He walked very stiffly, the men only a yard or two behind.

"I don't know why I did it. I have blackouts. I have terrible headaches," the prisoner was gasping. Tears were streaming down his cheeks; his hands were now raised as high as his shoulders. "Don't hurt me, please don't hurt me."

Then he looked up and saw Morrison.

And Morrison, with strange deliberation, put his hand into his pocket, took out an automatic pistol, and shot him—once through the forehead and once through the chest. The man must have died before he reached the ground.

10 The Murderer

Gideon, who was not a heavy drinker, was glad of his whisky that evening, and did not feel like drinking alone. Usually he would have called Hobbs in, but he was away, and there was no one else at the Yard with whom he felt like twenty minutes of relaxed shoptalk. A little after six o'clock, his notes unfinished, he called Information and said, "I'll be back in half an hour; tell the exchange," and went out. The day staff had already gone, except for a few stragglers. One girl, her skirt almost up to her bottom, went rushing along, completely oblivious. The constable on duty in the hall watched her flying down the stairs, turned, saw Gideon, and straightened up.

"Good night, sir."

"I'll be back in half an hour," Gideon said, his eyes twinkling, his spirits raised.

"Right, sir!" The other's eyes had a responding gleam.

Gideon walked down the long flight of stone steps. The time was coming, and was not far ahead, when he would be in the new building, urgently needed for years but, as an immediate prospect, not at all enticing. There was a warm familiarity about the Yard, even about this overcrowded courtyard itself, where cars were constantly coming and going, two traffic men were needed to keep it reasonably clear, and pedestrians had to be as alert as anywhere in London.

Tonight there was a slight, not unpleasant drizzle.

He passed the entrance to Cannon Row police station, part

81

of the buildings of the Yard but quite separate from it, and walked along Cannon Row to the pub which had stood there for over a century. He went into the saloon, where one junior and three senior detectives were standing at the bar. Over in a corner, by herself, Sabrina Sale sat bent over an evening paper, her eyes hidden behind her big, rimless spectacles. Gideon ordered a whisky-and-soda, and went straight across to her.

"May I join you?"

She looked up, startled.

"I—of course, Commander."

He saw that her glass was nearly empty.

"Can I get you another?"

She hesitated. "No. No, I don't think so; one is all I allow myself." She smiled. "Really, I mean it."

Gideon sat down, lifted his glass.

"Cheers."

"To a quiet evening," she said, and sipped her drink. "You don't often come in here, do you?"

"Not these days, no. Do you?"

"Most evenings during the week, just for a short time." She had a quiet, pleasant voice, and there was something about her which intrigued Gideon. Efficiency without fuss always attracted him. "I get tired by six o'clock, and can do with a slight boost."

"One does as one gets older," he said feelingly.

She gave a little amused smile. "Yes indeed!"

"How long have you been in the secretarial pool?" asked Gideon.

"Nearly a year," she answered. "I was with Traffic for years, and always hankered after your department, Commander."

"Think it would be more exciting?"

"More interesting," she corrected.

"Find it so?"

"Very much."

"Social conscience, or just a need for vicarious excitement?" Gideon asked.

"I don't think it's really either," answered Sabrina Sale thoughtfully. "I think I feel more part of Scotland Yard with the C.I.D., more part of a big machine. Am I being romantic?"

"There's nothing romantic about Scotland Yard!"

"What an absurd assertion," said Sabrina Sale crisply. "It's the most romantic place in the world."

He stared at her in amazement, saw that she was wholly serious, and did not know quite how to respond. He had a feeling that in some spheres he would soon be out of his depth with this woman, and began to wonder what impulse had made him join her. It was never wise to be oversociable with a member of the staff; too many, these days, took advantage of friendliness.

He said dryly, "One day when there's time, you'll have to explain that—so that I can tell my wife. I think she will be surprised!"

Sabrina didn't comment, but after a pause she asked, "Are you going back to the office?"

"Yes."

"You often work very late, don't you?"

"Inevitably."

"Now I think I understand," she remarked.

"Understand what?" asked Gideon.

"Why your wife mightn't feel that Scotland Yard is romantic!" On the instant, her face was wreathed in smiles and she leaned forward and touched his arm. "Don't take any notice of me, I'm only teasing. I suppose I mustn't ask why you're going back?"

"I've a memorandum to draft—you'll have it to type in the morning," answered Gideon. "I—"

The barman called out in a penetrating voice, "Commander Gideon. Is Commander Gideon here, please? . . . Wanted on the telephone!"

Gideon was already on his feet. He nodded to Sabrina Sale, whose gaze followed him for a moment before she picked up her paper again. He forgot her. There would be no call for him here at this hour unless it was really urgent. The telephone was in a small alcove on the other side of the bar. Several officers made a point of making way for him. The barman, obviously new, said, "Round there, sir." Gideon picked up the receiver, which was lying on its side.

"Gideon," he said.

"There's an urgent call for you from Richmond, sir," the operator said. "I'm holding them on the line."

"I'll nip across into Cannon Row," Gideon said "Put it through there." He hurried out, and stepped into the road—and a car horn blared. He drew back hastily, mouthed "sorry" to an indignant middle-aged driver, crossed more carefully, and reached the Cannon Row police station. There was a telephone in the hall, and he picked it up.

"Commander." It was Joe Moore. "We've had a—" He broke off, but already Gideon understood that he was off-balance and badly shaken, which was rare with a senior officer. Was it simply that the child's body had been found? Even an experienced man might feel shattered by such an experience, though it was unlikely he would show it. "I've slipped up very badly," Moore went on, and Gideon thought, He's let the killer escape. "We caught the man," went on Moore, in the same rather emotional way, "but I didn't think to have Morrison—the father—searched. I suppose I should have. Anyway, he shot him."

Gideon echoed, not fully comprehending, "He shot him. You mean—" He stopped as understanding flooded into his mind, a touch of horror accompanying it.

"The father shot the killer of his child," declared Moore with great deliberation. "In front of my eyes—with a hundred people looking on. I've had to charge him, Commander. Oh, why the hell did I let it happen?"

Gideon didn't speak for a moment; he could not. Already

84

the possible consequences of what he had been told were going through his mind and he was far from clear about the best thing to do—for Moore, for the police generally, for Morrison and his wife. The silence seemed to drag on for a long time, but suddenly he made up his mind.

"I'll come over," he said. "Where are you?"

"On the Common," answered Moore.

"Honiwell there yet?"

"No, but he's on his way."

"I'll join you as soon as I can." Gideon put the receiver down quickly, then lifted it again with hardly a pause. The Cannon Row operator answered. "Have you a line to the Back Room?" he asked.

"Yes, sir."

"Put me through, please."

The Back Room was the office of the Chief Inspector who was in direct liaison with the newspapers on any such case as this—any case under investigation, in fact. A crowd of reporters would be on the Embankment near the office, alert for any news. Gideon was through almost at once.

"Yes, Commander?" A slight Welsh lilt in the voice of the man who answered told Gideon he was speaking to Chief Inspector Huw Jones.

"Are they clamoring after you?" Gideon demanded.

"There must be at least twenty, sir! I've told them I'll have something for them in half an hour, but I can stall if I have to."

"Tell them I'll come around," said Gideon. "In five minutes, for five minutes. And tell Information I need a car for Wimbledon Common, at once."

He rang off, and was watched openly by two uniformed men, covertly by several others as he strode out. There was a short cut across the courtyard to the Back Room, which opened onto the Embankment itself, and he walked rapidly across it to the ground-floor entrance of the main building.

Everyone in the courtyard was aware of Gideon's progress. As he disappeared, a youthful detective sergeant remarked, "He must be well over fifty, and he moves as if he's jet-propelled."

No one scoffed.

Chief Inspector Huw Jones was tall, dark, thin-faced, with rather heavy-lidded eyes unexpectedly bright. He was most astute in evading questions from the press yet extremely popular with them. Whenever he could possibly let them have information quickly, he did. This evening, he had called them from the Embankment into a small room which was so packed that Gideon had to squeeze through the door to get inside. "I've told 'em they can take photographs," he whispered in Gideon's ear, and that seemed the signal for several flashlights to go off at once. Photographers were either at the front, too closely packed, or standing on chairs at the back.

There was almost complete silence, and a dozen men had pencils poised.

"I've got about three minutes left," Gideon said briskly. "I'm going over to Richmond to find out exactly what's happened. Meanwhile, you don't need telling that Superintendent Moore has done a remarkable job in catching the man Oliver so quickly. It was one of the quickest and best-organized manhunts we've ever staged, and I'm not exaggerating."

He paused.

"But he let Morrison shoot—" a man began.

"He didn't let anybody do anything," interrupted Gideon. "The only way he could have stopped that shooting was by stopping the father from searching for his own child—no one then knew she was dead, remember—or by getting him to turn out his pockets, and he'd no reason or excuse to do that."

From the back a man called out, "Are you whitewashing him, Commander?"

"Use your own judgment," Gideon retorted. "But use judgment, not prejudice." Several men laughed. "The most significant thing about the search is the speed with which it was organized. That wouldn't have been possible if the mother hadn't been very quick to report the child missing. The Division was ready and we had military help on the spot within the hour. If we'd lost any time, the man wouldn't have been caught."

Into a brief silence, a man spoke in a dry, sardonic voice. "And he would be alive, Commander."

"If we'd known even sooner, the girl might be alive, too," said Gideon. "Now I must go."

A dozen questions were flung at him as he turned and went out, and he heard Jones answering for him. The door closed, and he strode into the courtyard where a car was waiting with a driver at the wheel. Gideon got in behind the driver, and sat back. The car moved off with quiet speed, turned right onto the Embankment and right again at Big Ben. The evening rush hour was beginning to slacken off, but there was still plenty of traffic about. The drizzle had stopped; the sun was breaking through, and it gilded the gates of the Houses of Parliament and the newly cleaned stonework of the main buildings. The journey might take twenty minutes, but it was more likely to take thirty.

It did not now occur to Gideon to doubt that his approach to the press had been right. There would be implications that the police should have stopped the shooting, and obviously there was basic truth in that, but he'd done what he could for Moore and had emphasized the value of quick reporting to the police. But for the shooting, this case would have been very much on the credit side. The problem, as in all offenses of this kind, was for the Yard to be geared to the point of high efficiency necessary to combat a crime that was rare in comparison with others, but, in view of its horrifying aspects, committed far too frequently for the public to take calmly.

Just over twenty-five minutes later, Gideon was stepping out of the car onto the grass of the Common. At least a thousand people were gathered about in little groups, as if it were a sporting event. Joe Moore and Honiwell were together by the side of an ambulance, and Gideon knew that the bodies had been held there until he arrived. More cameras clicked; two movie cameras whirred, doubtless for the television newsrooms.

Gideon shook hands, first with Moore and then with Honiwell. The cameras went into a frenzy.

"Just show me around so that they can take a few pictures," Gideon said. "Everything's under control, isn't it?"

"Absolutely," Honiwell said.

"Now it is," Moore said bitterly.

"Where's the man Morrison?"

"I sent him to the Divisional station—he's in the cells," Moore answered.

"I'll see him there," decided Gideon, and they began to move about, still followed by the photographers and newspapermen. At least twenty police were forming a cordon to keep the rest of the crowd back. Gideon reached the ambulance and saw the two stretchers, their burdens covered with white sheets—the child who had been so cruelly murdered and the man who had been so mercifully shot.

Mercifully?

Another thought struck Gideon. An eye for an eye, a tooth for a tooth, a life for a life. Thousands, probably millions, of people would believe the father was justified in what he had done. Before the trial was over, the prolonged controversy over hanging would be split wide open again; great bitterness as well as shrieking lust for vengeance would be aroused.

At last the ambulance had driven off, and the routine work was done. And at last Gideon could turn to Honiwell and ask, "Could this be your man, too?"

"I doubt it—I doubt it very much," answered Honiwell gloomily. "I'm afraid my killer's still on the loose."

Gideon nodded.

As he was driven to the Richmond police station, where he would see Frank Morrison, he noticed a small transformer station standing well back from the road, the "Danger" notice, behind the strong wire fence, very clear. For the first time since he had been called from Cannon Row, his thoughts shifted off the murdered child to the cases of sabotage. He would see Piluski first thing in the morning; there was now no chance of seeing him tonight.

The street lights were on, as were those of the police station as he stepped inside. The press was present in strength again; there was nearly as large a crowd as there had been on the Common.

One of the reporters called out, "Can we have a statement, Commander?"

"We'll see," Gideon called back.

"Are you going to see Morrison?"

"Yes."

"You ought to let him go!" cried a little man at the front of the crowd. "You ought to let him go. He's a *hero*, he's not a murderer."

Someone else called out, "You shouldn't have arrested him."

"Let him go!"

"Bloody police—you can catch the *easy* ones!"

"A life for a life!" a woman screeched. "That's the law of the Bible; that's what it ought to be in Britain. *Let him go!*"

The cries faded as Gideon continued into the police station. He wasn't surprised by the sentiment; he *was* surprised at how strongly and quickly it was being expressed. There was a smack of professionalism about it, of having been laid on. If that was the case, then the organization of the "bring back the rope" supporters was very good indeed.

They went into Moore's big, tidy, brightly lit office with a map of Richmond and an enlarged map of Richmond Park on the walls.

"I need a drink," Moore said.

"I'll see Morrison right away," said Gideon. "Take me to him, Joe, will you?" He didn't say so but he did not want

Moore to have whisky on his breath when he talked to the press, as he would soon have to. "Then we'll see the press, then—"

As he spoke, the lights went out.

11 *Piluski Reports*

Gideon and the others stood absolutely still for perhaps three seconds. Sharp exclamations sounded and then faded. A man some distance off called, "Candles, quick!" Outside, the street lamps and lights at windows had gone out also. But the evening afterglow was strong, and gradually it was possible to see first silhouettes and then faces in some detail.

"If we're going to get this in September, what the hell's winter going to be like?" asked Honiwell.

"Had any blackouts here lately, Joe?" Gideon asked.

"One about a week ago, only lasted five minutes. I hope this one doesn't go on for long." Moore gave a bark of a laugh. "Keep the crowd quiet for a bit, anyhow. Commander, I can't tell you how sorry I am, or how grateful I am for what you're doing."

"Nothing to be grateful to me about," Gideon said gruffly.

"I know better, sir. You've come to draw their fire." After a pause, he went on, "I could find that whisky by sense of touch now."

"Leave it," Gideon said quietly. "Can you find your way down to the cells?"

Somewhere just outside the door, a match scraped and there was a flare of light; it faded but did not go out altogether; a steadier one brightened slowly. Torchbeams began to flash, and a man entered carrying a candle.

"Will two of these be enough for now, sir?"

"Are the cells lit, sergeant?" asked Moore sharply.

"We've lamps down there, sir, remember."

"I want to know if they're alight."

"Sure to be by now, sir."

"Let's go down and see," said Gideon.

Moore took a flashlight from his desk and led the way toward a flight of steps which Gideon remembered although he had not been there for years. The yellow rays of lamplight streamed out to meet them, so the sergeant was right. Three policemen were in the passage, opposite the cells. Gideon felt a glow of satisfaction, for the emergency arrangements had worked well and swiftly here; and the danger that Morrison might now attempt to kill himself had been anticipated.

Morrison was in the end one of three cells.

He sat, outwardly relaxed, on the narrow bed, feet stretched out, a newspaper in his hand. He had pushed the one pillow behind him and his head rested against the wall. He took no notice of the three men, even when the man who had been watching took out keys and rattled them as he opened the door.

Gideon went in first.

"Mr. Morrison?" he said tentatively.

The man on the bed turned his head at last. The strange thing, to Gideon, was that he seemed to be relaxed in mind as well as body, as if killing the murderer had drawn all the hatred and vengeance out of him. He looked rather tired.

"I haven't anything more to say," he said quietly. "I killed him. Such a man should not be allowed to live." His eyes widened slightly. "You're Mr. Gideon, aren't you?"

"Yes."

"Wouldn't you have done the same, if it had been your child?" Morrison demanded.

After a long, deliberate pause, Gideon answered, "I don't think so, Mr. Morrison. I hope not. But it isn't for us to show emotion or express opinions. We have to act according to the law. I understand you have refused legal aid."

"I don't need legal aid. The facts speak for themselves."

"I'd strongly advise you to have it, nonetheless," Gideon urged. "Is it a question of money?"

"Not entirely—I simply don't intend to defend myself," said Morrison. "I shall let the facts do that." He looked away. "I've no doubt my wife will need help, but I don't want to see her. Can you make her understand that?"

Gideon hardly knew what possessed Morrison; he stood looking down on this small man who was so composed, so absolutely convinced that he had done the right thing.

"So you are going to take your vengeance out on her, too, are you?" he asked. "A jury might understand what you've done so far, but very few human beings could understand what you propose doing to your wife."

Morrison's whole body stiffened. He stared penetratingly at Gideon, then turned away, did not look at him again, and would not speak. There was no point in staying longer, Gideon decided; Moore needed reassurance much more than Morrison did, and Gideon did not think there was the slightest danger that he might try to kill himself.

He deserved and needed so much sympathy, and yet in one way he made it difficult to feel any sympathy for him.

"If you ask me," said Moore, a little later, "I feel sorrier for his wife."

"She with friends?" asked Gideon gruffly.

"With her mother," answered Moore. "I'll go and see her soon. I'd like to get the press job over, Commander, so that I can have a drink."

As he finished speaking, the lights went on.

At that moment also, the lights went on in a small factory, only a half-mile away, and machines on the late shift began to hum again. Two electrician foremen made a hurried round of the factory, pressing down switches which had been turned off immediately the power cut had come. The night manager of the firm—a branch of Electronics New Age—picked up a telephone and called a number on the other side of London, the main factory near Barking.

"Mr. Roscoe, please," he said, and after a moment a man came on the line.

"Roscoe."

"We're in business again," the night manager reported with obvious satisfaction.

"Thank God for that," said Roscoe, who was the general manager. "How much production did we lose?"

"About ten per cent of the shift," the night manager answered.

Roscoe grunted, said, "Try to make it up," and rang off. Then he pulled some production graphs toward him and studied them closely. He was a scanty-haired man in his forties, and worry had engraved a permanent frown on his face.

Slowly, almost fearfully, he shook his head.

Honiwell, a big, endearing kind of man with curly brown-gray hair and a quiet voice, ate heartily of the casserole which Kate had prepared, drank beer, and talked. He obviously needed to talk, but he really hadn't much that was new to say. Everything that could be done in the Epping Forest search was being done, and until someone who knew the murderer came forward, there was little chance of getting him.

"Someone knows who it is, all right," he said. "How they can live with it, I don't know." He helped himself to more potatoes. "I must admit I'd like another job, George. I mean another assignment," he added hastily. "Anything going that would have a therapeutic effect on a kindly old uncle like me?"

The name "Entwhistle" flashed across Gideon's mind but he did not utter it.

"Hey, Dad!" It was Malcolm, at half past seven next morning. "You've got your picture in the paper! Can I come in?"

94

Kate slipped into a dressing gown, and called easily, "Yes, dear, of course."

Malcolm pushed the door open with his foot, and appeared with tea and two morning newspapers. Gideon was much less interested in his own photograph than in one which took up the whole of the front page of the *Daily Mirror*. It was almost unbelievable, perhaps the most dramatic picture he had ever seen.

A photographer had taken the picture at the exact moment that Morrison had shot Luke Oliver. In the expression of horror on Oliver's face, the way his hands were held upward and outward as if to fend the danger off, the picture was quite remarkable. Morrison's profile was set and he held his gun at arm's length. The thing which pleased Gideon, however, was the fact that two men just behind Morrison had grabbed him: one was actually touching his shoulder. They had been ready for a physical onslaught but were taken absolutely unaware by the shooting.

Who wouldn't have been?

"Everything's ready, sir," McAlistair said, an hour or two later. "Mr. Honiwell says you saw him last night. Mr. Brewer's got a new report on the Morden Bank robbery, and Mr. Hughes believes he has the man who robbed the Tottenham Post Office. He wants a warrant. Mr. Macintosh has the details of twenty-seven teen-agers caught smoking marijuana in a Hampstead cellar last night. Sir Humphrey Briggs called to say he's sorry but he can't improve on forty-eight hours with his report. Mr. Lemaitre will be calling about eleven o'clock. Mr. Piluski telephoned to ask if he could see you at two o'clock. Oh—and Mr. Hobbs is flying down from Scotland this afternoon."

That startled Gideon. "Did he say why?"

"He said the weather was very bad, sir."

Hobbs really meant that he knew Gideon had too much on his hands. Gideon gave an appreciative little smile, then glanced through the files and said, "I'll see Mr. Brewer."

There followed an hour and a half of intensive study of cases which were already preoccupying some of the C.I.D.'s best men. None of these was sensational or dramatic, none would rate more than a few inches of space in the newspapers, but all were representative of the average, everyday crime which the Yard investigated. The most worrying was the Hampstead drug case. It was difficult to see these drug-addicted youths, the hippies, the flower people, the love-ins, as part of the true pattern of modern society, but it was, and it was no use hoping that the craze would be short-lived. In certain ways, it grew stronger. One could be revolted by some of it, one could approve of some of it, but the Yard knew that it would be—in fact had long been —exploited by criminals. Catching an addict was easy; catching his supplier very different indeed. There was now much more overlapping of crimes than there had once been. To get their drugs, addicts stole. To spread their drugs wider, the suppliers traded on every form of human weakness. Gideon could see a whole new pattern of crime emerging, and it worried him, ' ut for the time being he could only cope with the evil which showed on the surface. He had finished just after eleven o'clock. At ten minutes past, Lemaitre telephoned, more brisk and slightly more self-assertive.

"We know young Jensen went to Jackie Spratt's Mill Lane office. A neighbor saw him. No doubt about it at all. But he wasn't seen to leave, George."

"What are you saying?" asked Gideon sharply. "That he didn't leave?"

"He certainly didn't after dark; we were watching too closely. And the neighbor says he didn't see anyone cycle away during the afternoon. The neighbor's an invalid, sits at the window all day."

"Did Jensen have a bicycle?"

"Oh, yes—that was his regular means of transport—got his initials on it, in green paint."

"Have you looked for the bicycle?" demanded Gideon.

"You bet your life we have. It's not at his home, nor at the youth club he goes to some nights. The one place it could be is behind Mill Lane. How about a general search for stolen bicycles in the area? If we went to Jackie's to find out if any of their employees had lost bicycles lately, we could go and look in the cycle sheds behind Jackie Spratt's place," Lemaitre suggested.

"Good idea," said Gideon.

"O.K., I'll get to it." There was a slight pause before Lemaitre went on: "Still taking it on the chin for us poor slobs who can't do our jobs, I notice. At least you got your picture in the paper!"

Gideon rang off.

He spent the next hour drafting his notes for the Ministry of Power and the industrialists, then sent for Sabrina Sale. She made no reference to the previous evening, looked—if anything—even more prim, and worked at the same high speed. Gideon gave her a bundle of correspondence, including his notes. "Let me have this back as soon as possible this afternoon," he said. "Let me know when you're coming, too. I'll make sure the window's shut."

She smiled pleasantly as she went out.

He worked solidly through reports until one o'clock, expected but didn't receive a call from Scott-Marle for details of the Morrison shooting case, had a sandwich lunch and coffee sent up from the canteen, and at two o'clock precisely expected Piluski.

And at two o'clock precisely, Piluski came in.

There was something intense about this man, about his deeply grooved face, and at this moment there was also a hint of satisfaction. He had seldom been in direct liaison with Gideon but now accepted the novelty of the situation without fuss, as a man superbly sure of himself, completely self-confident.

"We've started tackling this problem from the top,"

Gideon said, without preamble. "How have you been getting on from the bottom?"

"Would you like the general picture or the conclusion first, sir?" asked Piluski.

"The conclusion," Gideon answered.

"It *is* organized sabotage. It is done by various people, none of them yet known, who know exactly what they're doing. There are a lot of power stations in London which feed the current straight out to the consumers instead of going through the grid—and that's where the trouble's largely been. Most of the security men I've talked to see it entirely as a local problem—the theories go from a form of vandalism to a way of making overtime so as to get more pay, but one, at the New Bridge Station, has been doing some research on his own—he doesn't like what's going on at all."

"He's our man, then," said Gideon. "What's his name?"

"Boyd—John Boyd."

"The name vaguely rings a bell," Gideon said.

"He was with the Kenya Police Force for a while, was retired after independence, and took a job with the General Electricity Generating Board," replied Piluski. "He was at the Yard on a month's course when he was in the Kenya Force. What worries him most is the serious effect this could have in winter. It's bad enough now, but there's plenty of electricity in the grid, no problem in switching over once the need's obvious. That's what convinces him that it's skillfully organized, sir. Do you mind if I suggest you go to see him? You'll see what he's driving at much more easily if you're on the spot."

98

12 Powerhouse

Along the river, between West Ham and East Ham—thickly populated districts of London where the rows of small houses in drab narrow streets were dotted with big blocks of flats rising seven or eight stories high—was the New Bridge Power Station. Beyond it, nearer the outskirts of London, was the mass of industrial buildings ranged about East Ham, Barking, and Dagenham, where the giant Ford Company sprawled close to the river. Farther out still were the mud flats of the Thames Estuary, the Essex marshes, the North Sea, and Europe, but here among this conglomeration of homes and factories old and new, it was hard to believe that there was any world except the crowded streets and the narrow, straggling shopping centers. Here a big proportion of London's industry depended on electric power for its life. So the people depended on it, too. Gas could feed boilers, domestic cookers, refrigerators; could heat water, could serve in a hundred ways; and so could oil. But even these fuels depended on electricity to switch on and switch off valves and supplies, to start a flame or to douse it.

Gideon, at half past ten next morning, sat with Piluski in the back of the big Humber, driven by the man who had taken him to Richmond and Wimbledon Common only two days before. Perhaps the contrast with those green and pleasant places was the reason this area depressed him. He had never worked here, except as relief many years ago, and if there was a part of London that he didn't know well, it was this.

At the end of a long, straight street with houses on either side, he caught his first glimpse of New Bridge Power Station.

Two streets farther along, Piluski said to the driver, "Turn here."

This was another, almost identical street, and even fitful sunlight and the tapestry of shadows could not give it beauty. Yet as they drove along very warily—for toddlers by the dozen played on the narrow pavements and older children cycled precariously between curb and road—Gideon caught glimpses of beauty. Flowers in windows; here and there a house freshly painted; on the window sills of the first floors, flower boxes which caught the sun and made rainbows of their own. Brass letter boxes and knockers were brightly polished, steps to the front doors newly whitened. By the time he reached the power station, the sense of depression had gone.

New Bridge Power Station was neither new nor old. It was a little older than Battersea, with which Gideon was so familiar, and much newer than Lots Road. But New Bridge was more like Lots Road to look at: tall brick walls dark from its own smoke, the smoke of factory stacks and tens of thousands of tiny chimneys fed, even today, by hard fuel which sent its smuts and smog into the frowning skies.

Big notices on a wall said, "NO PARKING," "SLOW!" "DANGER," "DON'T BLOCK." The car reached the wall and turned left, opposite high green gates wide open. "SLOW!" was painted in huge letters on the gates, and "KEEP OUT UNLESS ON BUSINESS" only a little smaller. A man in uniform rather like the Port of London Authority Police stopped the car, saluted, and looked in.

"Commander Gideon for Captain Boyd," said Piluski.

"Oh, yes, sir. May I see your pass, please?" Piluski showed a green card. "Thank you. If you go between the two big buildings to the far end, you'll find an officer who will help you."

100

"Thanks," Piluski said. As he sat back, he remarked, "The building on the right is the generating station; on the other side are water storage tanks and boilers."

There was a deep, throbbing noise, much more noticeable than it had been from the gates, apparently coming from the generating shed. As they drove nearer, it became louder still. At the far end a big double door was open, and quite suddenly noise seemed to possess Gideon's whole body; throbbing smote his ears and seemed to quiver through every vein and nerve. Another man in uniform, sitting at a kind of sentry box, stood up as they approached.

"Oh, yes, gentlemen, Captain Boyd is expecting you. Parking Space Seventeen, please, and then a messenger will take you to the Captain's office."

Captain Boyd certainly had the situation under control.

As they got out of the car, the noise undoubtedly became greater, seeming to shake the ground under their feet. Gideon looked about him, seeing the high, grimy buildings, the mass of parked cars, a few workmen moving about, some brisk, some seemingly far too casual. There was a staircase leading to the side of the generating shed, and the door at the top open as Gideon looked up. A man appeared. He was in his forties, Gideon judged, big and powerful, and he moved very decisively down the steps. He wore a beige-colored suit which was somehow not quite right in this home of blacks and grays, dark greens and grimy whites. The sun caught his close-cropped, very fair hair.

"There's Boyd," Piluski said.

"I'll be at least an hour," Gideon said to the driver. "Get yourself some coffee." He moved off with Piluski as Captain Boyd reached the foot of the steps. Boyd was perhaps an inch taller than he, Gideon, and there wasn't much in it for breadth. Piluski was a pygmy compared with both men.

"Commander Gideon?" Boyd had a big, strong hand, a firm but not a crushing handshake. "I'm very glad to see

101

you." He had hazel eyes flecked with tawny brown; quite remarkable eyes. His features were craggy, and his skin shone, as if he had freshly shaved.

"Glad to see you, Captain Boyd. Will you lead the way?"

Boyd turned and went up very quickly. Gideon followed a little more sedately, looking down on a row of green-painted oil tanks, each one of which probably held a thousand gallons; at huge stacks of coal; at hundreds, probably thousands, of barrels, all holding fuel oil of some kind. Two huge stacks rose high above their heads.

The drumming noise grew louder, until Boyd opened the door at the top and Gideon stepped through.

It was like stepping into the eye of a hurricane. All about them was a fury of noise, a controlled howling, whining din; yet there was stillness. Down on the right, beyond a guardrail which reached shoulder height, were the enormous turbines, painted bright orange, utterly still and yet creating a strange impression of movement as well as power. Here and there stood white-smocked men, most of them with clipboards in their hands, while a few men in blue coveralls sauntered about. Beyond the generators was a huge wall of fuses, each as big as a telephone, each shiny white. Above this, and in the spider-like crisscross of steel girders in the roof, were neon lights, most of them giving a fair imitation of daylight.

Gideon could not prevent himself from pausing.

"New to you?" asked Boyd, close to his ear.

"I've been inside Battersea and Lots Road," said Gideon. "One forgets."

"Can you stand the noise?" Boyd's breath was warm on Gideon's cheek.

"Not if I can help it!" Gideon said clearly.

Boyd grinned, and opened a door opposite the guardrail. The wall in which the door was set seemed thin, but once it closed, much of the noise was shut out. There was still plenty, but it was no longer necessary to shout. A long, narrow passage led straight from the main door, with doors on either side, glass-paneled at the top. The walls here were glass, too, or plastic-paneled, so that dozens of men and women, all at desks, were visible.

"We call this the goldfish bowl," said Boyd. He had big, well-shaped teeth, which made his smile seem a little mechanical. Yet there was something appealing as well as impressive about him. "Here's where I live." He opened another door, the first one that was of solid wood, into another room, the sides of which appeared to be of glass. But there was hardly a sound as he closed this door, only a distant humming and throbbing. The office was sparsely furnished with steel chairs and filing cabinets. Along one wall ran a table which was obviously used as a control panel; Gideon could not see immediately what purpose it served.

"Sit down, please," said Boyd, and he sat behind a big, flat-topped desk when the others were seated. "Commander, I can't tell you what a proud moment this is in my life. I didn't ever expect to meet the most renowned detective in the world."

"Oh, nonsense," said Gideon, too startled to feel embarrassed.

"It isn't nonsense, Commander. I've been all over the world, and seen fifty different police forces in action, and they all speak of you with awe. I'm a little in awe of you myself, in point of fact."

"You conceal it well," said Gideon mildly.

"Conceal—" Boyd laughed loudly: he was in many ways a loud and boisterous man. "Your point, sir! If I hadn't already been in awe, I would very soon have become so after a talk with Superintendent Piluski here."

Piluski sat unmoving, almost as if he were carved from a particularly hard and dark wood.

"Why?" asked Gideon.

"I wouldn't have believed that anyone outside the industry would have spotted what you spotted so quickly. Most of my experience of the Establishment is that they wake up to what

103

might happen about a year after it *has* happened. What put you on to it?"

Whether he held Gideon in awe or not, he had certainly started as if he meant to take and keep the upper hand. Gideon thought he saw why he had been persuaded to come, rather than have Boyd visit him at the Yard. Boyd liked to be the dominant figure and was unwilling to risk the chance of being cut down to size.

"Thirty-five years of training, and the fact that I have to do a dozen things at once," he answered at last.

Boyd seemed to take this hint, for when he spoke it was in a rather different key, as if he were implying, All right, let's get down to business.

"Do you know the fundamentals of a generating plant?" he demanded.

"I've only a passing knowledge. Better assume I know nothing."

"Right, Commander! Then we heat the water which gives off the steam which drives the generator which feeds the network or the grid. This power goes out into the consumer lines through transformers which take it down from roughly 33,000 volts to 415 or 240. That boils your kettle."

Gideon nodded, impressed by the simplicity and the lucidity.

"To heat the water we need fuel and boilers, to work the transformers and to open and close valves and to control pressures we need electricity," Boyd went on. "There are a dozen ways in which we can have trouble, a dozen ways in which there can be a power failure, but the experts anticipated that. Consequently, they created a system by which if we get power failure from one source, another feed supply automatically comes in—*if* all the necessary valves, trips, and gadgets work, that is. Generally they do. Generally, I say —but there is still a ten-million-to-one chance of an accumulative series of breakdowns like they had in New York in 1965—or was it '66? A breakdown in power supply only comes if peak demands are made on it, or if there's interference. The interference is usually accidental or natural—act of God, so to speak—and can be quickly traced and put right. It is nearly always with transmission, occurring after the power has left the powerhouse or generating station. Cables or lines can be damaged, but the point is it's almost impossible to have a power failure of the kind we've been having lately unless two things go wrong at the same time. It can happen—it has happened. But not six or seven times in a row, within a short period. One or two failures could have been caused out of spite or for personal reasons, but this—" Boyd broke off, then added vehemently, "Not on your life!"

There was no doubt of the depth of his feeling, and there seemed to be none of his competence.

"You don't have to convince us of that," Gideon remarked. "What we have to find out is who's doing it, and why. If we don't stop it soon, it could really become dangerous."

"That's a major point of agreement between us," Boyd declared. "*I* think it's politically inspired."

"Why?" asked Gideon.

"It's the kind of thing that political fanatics would do."

"Might do, perhaps," Gideon conceded. "There are other possibilities." He did not feel inclined to elaborate, for he had become a little unsure of the man. "Have you had any trouble here?"

"No, thank God. And ever since it started, I've had a double and treble check at all danger points. One thing I should have told you. We're like most of the other London stations but not like the provinces. They feed the grid and the grid feeds the consumer. We feed the consumer and if we get in trouble, the grid feeds us. Some of the other big metropolitan areas are rather the same, I'm told, but my worry is London. We've four weak spots. The electrical supply itself. The water intake for the boilers. The valves which control the flame which heats the boilers. And the transmission, once the power's generated. No one can fool around with anything in this establishment without being seen and questioned."

"But they could have, before you learned what was happening in the other powerhouses."

"Yes, sir! If the others would take the same precautions as we're doing, the saboteurs would run into trouble. Sooner or later someone's going to try here, and when we catch 'em—" He brought the palms of his hands together with a tremendous bang.

Gideon made no comment, but asked, "Now I'm here, may I have a look at these danger points?"

"There is a wonderful vantage point here," answered Boyd. "Quite by chance, too. This office used to be the wages office, but soon after I came I saw how it could be used—from this spot you can see pretty well every key point. Look."

He got up and led the way to the window behind him.

It was strangely placed, between the two big buildings, and he could see into the vast generating shed and the boiler houses on the other side. A telescope on a revolving stand had been erected at head height, so that Gideon did not have to bend down. Once he had his eye on it, the whole picture was transformed—even the farthest corner seemed close at hand. Certain spots had been marked with Day-Glo red paint, and these were obviously the danger points. Valves and switches had been ringed around, and the approach to them obviously cleared.

Boyd was giving a running commentary.

"If the oil lead to boilers one, two, and three was interrupted, the flame would fade, heat would be lost, and the steam pressure would soon start falling. So the turbogenerators would stop working and we'd be in bad trouble—we couldn't feed the railways. If boilers four, five, and six were affected, there'd be short supply to most of the industry we feed—and that's a lot of industry. We'd turn over automatically to the grid *unless* someone dickered around with that inflow. That's what's happened before: trouble in the powerhouse, simultaneous trouble with the grid inflow—result blackout.

"Take it from me, Commander, you can do a million pounds' worth of damage in five minutes." Boyd banged his hands together again. "In five minutes—in five *seconds*. If anyone wants to bring this nation to its knees, that's the way to do it. Cut out its *power*."

13 *The Cool Mind*

When Boyd stopped, the silence in the office was absolute.
Gideon could hear his own breathing, his heart thumping.
Gradually, sound came into his consciousness from outside.
That ceaseless drumming and throbbing, the very sound of
power. He studied the curiously feline eyes before him, the
rugged face, the shiny skin. He had seen men look like this,
occasionally, when they were carried away by some great
enthusiasm. It was the look of the fanatic and also the look
of the prophet.

It faded slowly.

Piluski spoke for the first time.

"Then it is even more important to find out who is behind
it, and why."

"You never said a truer word," agreed Boyd heartily. The
glow had quite gone, and the hint of fanaticism with it. He
took out a pale brown handkerchief and wiped his brow, then
peered into the telescope and swiveled it around slowly.
Gideon had a feeling that he was deliberately stalling, as if he
needed time to recover inwardly from the outburst. Piluski
looked intently at Gideon, his heart-shaped mouth pursed; it
made him look older.

Boyd moved from the telescope.

"How about some coffee?" he suggested. "Or something
stronger?"

"Coffee will be fine," Gideon said. "But I'd like a look
through the station before I go."

"Then let's do that now and come back for refreshment," said Boyd. "Shall I lead the way?"

He turned right, out of the door into the passage—the opposite direction from which they had come. The passage ended at a T-junction, and on the right was a small iron spiral staircase—surely a relic from a building which had been here long before this one. Boyd's footsteps rang out; he obviously wore metal tips on his heels. At the bottom of the staircase there were two doors, and he opened the one on the left.

Gideon was prepared for a sudden onslaught of sound, but there was very little. They entered an enormous room, or shed, which towered above their heads, turning them into midgets. Moving about leisurely were men in blue coveralls, some on platforms which ran halfway around the huge white-painted boilers. It was warm; not overhot but moistly warm.

"Here's the boilerhouse I was talking about," said Boyd. "It holds some of the biggest and most modern boilers in England. They hold 30,000 gallons—300,000 pounds in weight that is—and they produce three and a half million pounds of steam every hour."

Gideon tried to take this in as Boyd went on, "Very terrifying stuff, steam, when you come to think of it. Got far more power in it than we realize." He stood craning his neck to see to the top. "Get a buildup of steam pressure in one of those, close up the safety vent, and you could jam it easily—you'd blow the place to pieces."

"The place—or the boiler?" inquired Gideon.

Boyd looked at him almost pityingly.

"If one of those boilers exploded, there wouldn't be any boilerhouse left, worth speaking of. See those vents? The things that look like big doors?" There were two on the side of the boiler where they stood. "If there is a pressure buildup inside and a blow, the pressure blows them open and most of the steam is wasted. Makes a hell of a bang, and a hell of a blast, but no one's likely to get hurt and damage can soon be put right. Checking those safety vents is A-1 priority. I have instituted an hourly check."

"Can they jam accidentally?" asked Gideon.

"Not likely! No, Commander, if one of those was jammed it would be done deliberately. And the most likely way to cause an explosion *is* deliberate, too. Shut off the oil feed, put out the flame, leave it a few minutes, light the flame again, and up she'd go. Or play around with the water supply. If you cut that for a few minutes but maintain the heat, the boiler will get too hot and upsadaisy again. That's why I say *two* things have to coincide to make trouble. You can have an explosion in a boiler but it won't be serious unless the safety vent is jammed. Seen enough?"

"What fuel do you use here?"

"In this house, heavy oil. There's a smaller house next door which uses solid fuel, but the principle's the same. The oil feed goes straight into the burner, which ignites the gases; the solid fuel goes into a hopper and then into a mill which crushes it to powder—fine as face powder, that stuff, ought to be a commercial market in our new ghettos! The powder's not so different from the oil; the principle's the same."

He strode on—pointing at electric switches, complicated-looking valves and equipment at the foot or side of each boiler, repeating monotonously, "Electricity again—see how dependent we are on it? Throw the wrong switch and we can be in serious trouble. That's a safety valve which shuts out automatically, but it can be jammed, and without current it wouldn't work. . . . Go through this door into the yard."

They went out into the cool fresh air of the morning—and Gideon had a sense almost of surprise. It was so bright and sunlit, so normal. He had not realized when they were inside how oppressive the boilerhouse had been. They walked along a hard-surfaced road between storage tanks on one side and the thousands of drums on the other.

"Oil storage—and some emergency supplies in drums could get us out of trouble if there are holdups in delivery. We carry only a week's supply, so a strike by oil delivery men could cause chaos, especially in the winter," Boyd said. "This way."

110

They turned in to a narrow alley, where there was no room for a car to pass. At the far end was an open shed with bicycle racks, comparatively few of the racks filled. Gideon thought of Lemaitre and the missing George Jensen and his bicycle, but that did not stay in his mind for long.

John Boyd did.

Boyd led the way, a tremendously powerful man striding with an almost tiger movement; blond beast, Gideon thought, out of nowhere. He led the way across the road between the powerhouses and the generating shed. Doors leading into the shed were heavily marked: "KEEP OUT UNLESS ON BUSINESS." "SHOW YOUR PASS." "DANGER." By each door was one of the uniformed security men, and the nearest moved forward very quickly when Boyd turned toward his door.

"Going in, sir?"

"Yes." Gideon had a feeling that Boyd added, "You fool," under his breath. The door opened and they stepped into a kind of sound trap which reminded Gideon of the entrances to air-raid shelters during the war. Though noisier here than outside, it was not deafening. The droning, throbbing sound of power seemed muted. Then Boyd opened another door, and the roar thundered against their ears with ferocious impact. Gideon felt as if he had come up against a wall of raging sound.

From ground level, the turbogenerators, painted in that bright orange, looked like grotesquely swollen slugs hugging the cement floor. There was vibration everywhere, faint but unmistakable, as if some uncontrollable convulsion were shaking the earth. There seemed to be a latent threat that the vibration would grow fiercer and fiercer until finally it shook the very strength out of all those who were rash enough to be near.

The men looked so tiny, so ineffective, yet they moved about with a kind of calculated precision, without haste but with clearly understood purpose. Two men in business suits came out of an office, but did not approach the trio.

111

"This is where we can run into more trouble," declared Boyd. He directed his voice well, so that he could be heard clearly. "This is the panel which controls distribution to the various centers." He led them to the high wall on which the telephone-size "fuses" were fastened. Each was marked with the name of a company or place. "B & I Cables," read one; "Ford's—Emergency," "Hospital," "Technical College," "Power Electrical," "Race Track." In all there must be over a hundred, Gideon estimated.

"Pull one of these out, blow it, cut a wire, or switch off the current—and the supply fails," went on Boyd. "Damage the whole control board, and there will be a blackout over the entire area. The grid can cut in quickly, but if there's simultaneous trouble at the transmission lines from the grid, then power's off for an hour, maybe a lot longer. I tell you this place is as vulnerable as a bank, Commander."

"I realize that," Gideon said.

"Then you're the first man I've come across in any position of authority to do so," said Boyd. "That's a lot of responsibility on your shoulders."

"Can you give us any positive clue as to the identity of the saboteurs?" inquired Gideon.

"Look among the Commies and the militant immigrant groups," urged Boyd. "And look among the Campaign for Nuclear Disarmament sissies and those humbugging flower people. You know what I think, Commander?" He gave Gideon no chance to answer as he careered on. "This country is ripe for revolution. It may sound corny to say that the first thing revolutionaries would go for is power, but I mean *this* kind of power. If they could get control of it, or put it out of action for a few days, they'd be halfway home. *I* think these powerhouses ought to be put on a military security basis."

Gideon made no comment.

Boyd gave a fierce grin, and said in a very loud voice, "When I first warned them what was going to happen in Kenya if they didn't police the country better, they ignored me. I was right then. I'm right now. I can't make you or anyone else see it, can't make a horse drink even when you've led it to the water. But one thing's certain."

He pushed open a door on the other side of the great shed, and they stepped into another sound trap, then outside into the bright morning. Gideon had been so intent on what Boyd was saying that he had almost forgotten the throbbing and droning of the turbogenerators. Here the quiet brought him up sharply to the point of realization.

The door closed, and Boyd went on as if there had been no interruption. One of the uniformed security men moved aside to let them pass.

"There won't be any trouble at New Bridge; you can be sure of that. *I* won't let it happen. But this is only one of twenty-odd stations in the Greater London area, Commander. Failure at any one of the others could do a lot of harm. Whole areas can be blacked out at will—but I don't need to rub that in, do I?"

"No," Gideon said. "You certainly don't."

Boyd clapped his hands together; for the first time he failed to trap enough air between his palms, and the sound was a faint echo of the resonant bangs he had made before. Gideon saw his car about a hundred yards away, the driver talking to a security guard, so they had come full circle.

"Have you approached anyone else about this?" Gideon asked.

"I've told my masters what I think."

"About what, precisely?"

"The vulnerability of all power stations and the need for much stricter security."

"Have you told them why you think so?"

"No, sir!" answered Boyd, his grin holding more than a touch of derision. "They would think I was a crank. I tell 'em what could happen; you're the man to find out why. I shouldn't think anyone else can."

They stopped by the side of the car.

"If I get any news worth passing on, I'll tell you," Gideon said. "Superintendent Piluski will get in touch with you in person."

He put out his hand, and Boyd took it firmly, holding it a few seconds longer than convention demanded.

"We're relying on you," he said. "We really are. Thanks for coming." He shook hands with Piluski, and then turned and strode off toward the staircase down which he had come when Gideon had first seen him.

Gideon and Piluski got into the car. Security men watched them out, and soon they were driving along the narrow streets, with the tall stacks of the power station behind them casting a kind of shadow. The children still played and the older ones still cycled.

Gideon, noticing this, said almost casually, "Shouldn't these children be at school?"

"There's a teachers' strike in this part of London," Piluski told him.

"Oh, yes, I'd forgotten." Gideon sat back, feeling a strange kind of relaxation, as if he were recovering from a period of great exertion, although in fact he had little more than walked and listened. Then he chuckled. "There's another thing that got forgotten. Our coffee!"

"Great Scott!" exclaimed Piluski. "Boyd will kick himself when he realizes that!"

"I'm not at all sure that Captain John Boyd ever reaches that point of annoyance with himself, if any point," remarked Gideon dryly. "What we've got to check is whether he's right."

"About the political implications, do you mean?"

"Yes—and about the vulnerability." For the first time, Gideon began to feel anxious to see the Minister of Power, and to find out what the CBI reaction was going to be. "Why did you want me to go to New Bridge instead of having him come to see me?"

Piluski shot him a quick, wry smile.

"Seen in the Yard or against any other background, he's so much larger than life that he wouldn't seem real, sir. Against the power station, he's real enough and you can see what makes him so apprehensive. Don't you agree it was better to meet him there?"

"Yes," Gideon said. "Put the details of the interview in as part of the general report, will you?"

"Yes, sir," promised Piluski. "I'll do it tonight."

They sat in silence for a few minutes, driving toward Poplar. Soon they would be in the City. Traffic was heavy, particularly the big trucks from the docks which ranged along the river on their left. Now and again through gaps in the buildings, they could see the cranes at the wharves. It passed through Gideon's mind that one of the power stations must feed the docks, that a failure there could affect cranes, loading and unloading—all the activity of the docks with all its significance for London's people.

There was no doubt about the vital importance of the power stations. But surely those in authority knew that; they didn't need a domineering, power-conscious man like Boyd to tell them.

Did they?

There was a voice over the car radio, and Gideon sat up to listen as the driver said, "Commander Gideon's vehicle."

"Is Commander Gideon there?"

Gideon leaned across and took the speaker.

"Yes, speaking."

"Mr. Hobbs for you, sir," Information said, and after a pause Hobbs came on. He hadn't lost a minute getting from the airport, Gideon thought appreciatively. He had a clear, cultured voice, quite unhurried. Nothing could have sounded less like Boyd's.

"You have a three-o'clock appointment at Millbank, Commander," he said, and Gideon knew at once that he meant with the Minister of Power. "Shall I confirm it?"

"Yes," said Gideon. "How long have you been there?"

"About half an hour."

"Thanks for coming back," Gideon said, glancing at his watch. It wanted a few minutes to twelve. "I'll be at the office shortly."

"There's one other thing," said Hobbs.

"Yes?"

"A Reverend Josiah Wilkinson is here, and says he will sit in the hall until you see him," said Hobbs. "He's one of the prison visitors at Dartmoor. He won't tell me what he wants to talk to you about, but he knows you by sight. If you don't want him to know you're back, you might be wise to come in the other way."

Gideon grunted. And he got the impression that Hobbs felt sympathetic toward the Reverend Josiah Wilkinson. Any prison visitor at Dartmoor almost certainly knew Geoffrey Entwhistle, he reflected.

"I'll see him," he said. "But warn him I can't spare more than fifteen minutes or so."

It did not seem strange to him that he should be called on to switch so suddenly from a subject of mass significance to the affairs of a single man. It was part of his job.

14 Prison Visitor

Gideon walked past the clergyman who sat at the window in the hall, without glancing at him. Nevertheless, his impression was clear enough. And he was surprised. The name "Josiah Wilkinson" had conjured up a vision of an elderly or at least old-fashioned parson, but this man appeared to be somewhere in his early thirties, and looked a healthy, outdoor type. He stared intently at Gideon, but did not speak or attempt to attract his attention. Gideon went into his office, where several notes, all in Hobbs's handwriting, were awaiting him. Already he felt that things were under control.

The first note read: "Frank Morrison remanded in custody for eight days."

The second: "Lemaitre reports G.J.'s bicycle was at a secondhand shop in Brick Street."

The third: "Autopsy on Sheila Morrison tomorrow, Friday, 2 P.M. Do we want an observer?"

The fourth: "Sir Humphrey Briggs's report delayed another 24 hours—with his apologies."

The fifth: "Chief Fire Officer Carmichael suggests lunch tomorrow, 12.45 for one o'clock, R.A.C. Club."

The sixth: "Commissioner telephoned for you at 11.30 and 12.05."

Gideon put these aside and pressed the bell to Hobbs's room. After a pause, the door opened without the jack-in-the-box violence Gideon had become used to, and Deputy Commander Hobbs came in. He was a quiet, controlled man,

117

good-looking in a rather negative way, dark-haired, dark-eyed. His background was very much public school and university, and for many years Gideon had doubted whether such a springboard would enable him to hold a senior post at the Yard, for the men with whom he worked and the habitual criminals talked a different language. Hobbs, knowing this, had learned theirs without in any way making concessions or trying to adjust to them. He had spent some time in N.E. Division, where Lemaitre was now in charge, and he had done a better job than Lemaitre. He was a dedicated detective, bringing an excellent mind and up-to-date training to bear on all police problems. It had taken a long time for him and Gideon to establish full understanding, but they had it now. Indirectly this had been due to the overriding tragedy in Hobbs's life: the death, after much suffering, of his wife. Somehow this had done much to bring out the depth of humanity and humility in him, qualities which had been over-lain by a certain aloofness of manner and the habit of keeping his thoughts as well as his anxieties to himself.

Now he looked rested, tanned, well.

They shook hands.

"Thanks again," Gideon said.

"I was getting tired of shooting grouse, anyhow," said Hobbs. His gaze, quite impersonal, was very direct. "You're looking tired. It's time you got away for a week or two."

"Not until this latest business is over," said Gideon. "When did you hear about the appointment with the Minister?"

"The Commissioner spoke to me when he couldn't get you," Hobbs said. "I called you immediately. It's to be a confidential person-to-person talk."

"Good."

"And there is a meeting with the CBI tomorrow morning —that's just been confirmed. What's it all about?"

"Blackouts," Gideon said.

"I remember you were preoccupied about them before I

left," said Hobbs. "So there have been more."

"Yes." Gideon stared out over the river for a few moments, and then went on, "Ever heard of John Boyd, now security chief at New Bridge Power Station?"

"Yes," answered Hobbs promptly. "I met him out in Kenya soon after I joined the Force. A team of us went out to study conditions. And I've met him once or twice since, too, on special inquiries. He's a good all-round policeman."

Gideon asked, "Sure?"

Hobbs frowned, then amended slowly, "I think I see what you mean. He's a good all-round detective, but I seem to recall that some of his political opinions might be too strong for him to be objective. I haven't seen him for several years. He may have got more vehement."

"Taking your opinion as correct, he certainly has," said Gideon ruefully. "I'd like to learn more about him. Ask the Special Branch if they know anything, and put somebody onto him—political associations, personal life, everything. Don't tell Piluski about this yet. I'd like this to be something quite separate, and if Piluski knows what I'm doing he might inadvertently give something away. Boyd's nobody's fool."

"I'll fix it," promised Hobbs.

"Now, what about this parson?"

Hobbs smiled.

"He was sitting there when I came in, and the duty sergeant said he wouldn't budge, so I had a word with him. But he says what he has to say is highly confidential and that he must see you."

"No idea what it's about?" asked Gideon.

"None at all."

"Remember Geoffrey Entwhistle?" Gideon said, and saw Hobbs's look of surprise.

"He's at Dartmoor!"

"That's right." Gideon went to his own desk, took out the brief note from Entwhistle, and handed it to Hobbs, who scanned it, handed it back, and said with obvious self-reproach, "I should have made him talk to me. You don't want to be worried by this kind of thing."

"It's just the kind of thing that should worry me," Gideon replied. He put back the note and laughed with mild amusement. "It will be funny if it's about something else. Have him sent in, will you?"

Hobbs said, "Yes," and went out.

Gideon forced his thoughts back to the Entwhistle case, so that he would be wholly familiar with it by the time Josiah Wilkinson arrived. He had thought then, and thought now, that if it could have been established by the defense that Entwhistle's wife had had a lover, it would have cast sufficient doubt on the evidence for there to have been an acquittal. He could remember Entwhistle well—a very much less aggressive and less positive John Boyd to look at. Same kind of coloring, same kind of rangy figure.

There was a tap at the passage door.

"Come in."

"Mr. Wilkinson, sir," a messenger said.

Full-face, Josiah Wilkinson looked even younger than Gideon had thought, certainly the youngest prison visitor he had ever known, except in Borstal and in detention centers for young people. He had clear gray eyes and a spotlessly scrubbed look.

"Very good of you to see me, Commander," he said as he sat down. "I'm sorry I was so insistent."

"It's often the only way to get what you want," said Gideon.

"It is indeed! I wouldn't have come but for the fact that I've been assured that you can be absolutely objective—even about any mistake you may have made in the past."

"I'm glad I've got that reputation," Gideon said dryly.

"Both the Governor at Dartmoor and the Chief Constable have assured me that it's more than a reputation. Let me get to the point, Commander. I believe there has been a grave miscarriage of justice, and I've come to the conclusion that the police are the only people who might be able to put it right. I've studied this aspect of the law very closely. In my younger days, I tried very hard to get certain cases reopened, but the 'usual channels' are choked with red tape and precedent."

"I'm often told that about Scotland Yard," Gideon said gravely, checking a smile at his youthful-looking visitor's reference to his "younger days." "Who is the person involved?"

"A Geoffrey Entwhistle. I believe you've heard from him recently."

"Yes." Gideon smiled. "You put him up to writing and then came to follow up the impact of his note. Is that it?"

Wilkinson looked startled—and then he chuckled.

"Absolutely right," he confessed. "Do you remember the case?"

"Very well indeed."

"Are *you* convinced that justice was done?"

"I'm convinced that, as in every murder investigation, the case was only presented in the absolute conviction that the evidence was conclusive," Gideon answered carefully.

"That hardly answers my question, surely."

"Mr. Wilkinson," said Gideon, "this isn't a cross-examination, and I have limited time. I don't yet know whether I should or whether I can help. How did Entwhistle convince you that he was innocent?"

"The absolute unvarying similarity of his story whenever he told it to me," said Josiah Wilkinson. "I am supposed to be a softening influence in the prison—to win privileges and concessions which others won't give. I am not so young or gullible as I look, however." He was quite serious, although he was smiling. "I have heard the plea of innocence a hundred times, and never before been convinced—it is almost invariably made in the hope of getting extra remission, or other privileges. So whenever I hear a new one, I ask questions about it out of the blue—jump into the middle of the

121

story, say, or pick up some trifle that isn't significant in itself. In the past, this has always caught the complainant out in positive lies, but I've never caught Entwhistle out. I could tell you exactly what he did on the night when he came home and found his wife murdered, what he did afterward, exactly how he felt. I do not believe he killed his wife, Commander."

"Nor do you believe that you've enough evidence to ask to have the case reviewed," said Gideon shrewdly.

"No, Commander, I'm afraid not. I am sure the Home Secretary would refuse. I've no actual new evidence to offer, and an instinctive conviction is hardly a legal argument."

"It certainly isn't," agreed Gideon, but his tone was gentle. The more he saw and listened to Josiah Wilkinson, the more he liked him. "So you come to me, knowing *I* can't reopen the case without instructions. Why? My reputation for objectivity wouldn't impress the Home Secretary any more than your instinctive conviction."

Wilkinson was silent for a long time, and then said, "Yes, it would, Commander."

"In what way?" asked Gideon, unmoved.

"If *you* were to report that you had found indications that there might be fresh evidence, he would listen to you."

"But I have found no such indications," Gideon said.

"I think I can give them to you," replied Wilkinson flatly.

"What are they?" demanded Gideon.

"One of the Entwhistle children, the youngest, remembers the mother talking about going to see a very special friend," said Wilkinson. "I've tried to urge her to tell me more, but she seems to withdraw into some inner fastness of her own. I believe she could be made to talk by a psychiatrist, but I'm not sure it would be a good thing for her. On the other hand, if the existence of a lover could be proved it would indicate the possibility of a different motive, wouldn't it?"

Gideon looked at him thoughtfully, but didn't speak.

"I've seen the child half a dozen times, at the home of the aunt and uncle who took them in," Wilkinson continued. "I

122

went there first simply to visit them, because Entwhistle was very anxious to find out how they are getting on. The youngest child, Carol, worried me from the first."

"Why?" demanded Gideon.

Wilkinson frowned. "She's taken the loss of her parents very hard. She doesn't play with other children, doesn't lead a normal life at all. Her uncle and aunt—they took all three children in—are very worried. They've seen doctors, but no one is able to help."

Again Gideon paused, and then said quietly, "Yet this is the one who talks of remembering her mother going to see a very special friend. She was four or five at the time, hardly the most reliable age for memory. And a special friend could mean anybody—"

"Exactly!" interrupted Wilkinson. "*Anybody*—including a lover. Commander, it is a terrible thing to live with the possibility that someone is in prison for the crime of murder, which he didn't commit. I've talked to all the children, of course. Clive, the eldest, pretends it doesn't worry him, but the pretense is too brittle to be true; Jennifer has moments of fierce defiance that sometimes lead to taunts from other children. The position is terrible enough in all conscience, but if their father is innocent, how much worse."

Slowly, heavily, Gideon said, "Yes, I see exactly what you mean."

Wilkinson did not speak.

Gideon watched him, pondering. He would not have felt as he did had there not been that tinge of doubt in his own mind, and now he was wondering what he might possibly do. Wilkinson was quite right: the case certainly couldn't be reopened unless there was positive evidence, but how could positive evidence be obtained if the police didn't look for it? On the other hand, was there really any justification for expecting—even hoping—to find it now, when none had been found at the time of the case?

The Yard *had* tried to find out if there had been a lover,

but—had they tried hard enough? It hadn't, strictly speaking, been their job—rather the job of the defense. It was no use allowing sentiment to influence him, or the persuasion of this earnest young man who had described the children's plight with such graphic realism.

He leaned forward.

"What is your interest in the case, Mr. Wilkinson? Why are you exerting yourself so much?"

Wilkinson pushed back his chair and placed his hands on the arms, almost as if the question offended him.

"Must there *always* be a motive for what one does, Commander?"

"Yes," said Gideon flatly.

"Must there *always* be something 'in it for me'? Do you really—"

"Now, steady on," protested Gideon. "I didn't ask you whether *you* were getting anything out of it. I simply want to know why you're doing it. Entwhistle was a complete stranger to you when you first met at Dartmoor, I imagine?"

"He was. He was not even a man I greatly liked," answered Wilkinson, much more mildly. "But I've come to like him and to believe in him. My motive is simply to try to help a man and his children, in the face of a very grave human problem. After all, that *is* what I'm supposed to do—paid to do as a minister of religion, if it comes to that. I suppose you could say that I'm simply doing my job in the best way I know how."

15 The Minister

Gideon sat very still, and Wilkinson sat exactly as he was, hands on chair arms, as if ready to get up. The room seemed unnaturally quiet; only sounds of traffic outside disturbed it. Many thoughts passed through Gideon's mind, the most vivid perhaps that Wilkinson might be his own son in age, and was not unlike Tom, his eldest boy—long since married and away from home. The next most urgent thought was that he must not raise this man's hopes—or Entwhistle's—in the slightest degree.

Quietly he said, "I'll give you this assurance, Mr. Wilkinson. I will go over the files, discuss the case with the investigating officers concerned, and try to find a flaw in what we did. If there is such a flaw, then I will examine it in order to find out if there is enough justification for us to reopen the investigation." He saw Wilkinson's eyes light up, and went on, "But I'm not hopeful. And I'm promising nothing beyond that."

"Precisely what *are* you promising?" asked Wilkinson, and then added hastily, "This is for my own satisfaction. I should not of course tell Entwhistle."

"It would be very cruel if you did," Gideon remarked, but he was facing the fact that Wilkinson was doing his best to make him commit himself. "I am promising you that if I find anything in a re-examination of our investigation to suggest that anyone at the Yard made a mistake, I will try to rectify it. It could—I'm a long way from saying anything stronger—

it could possibly throw some doubt on the verdict. If we at Scotland Yard informed the Home Office that *we* thought there was a miscarriage of justice, the Home Secretary would not ignore us."

"No," breathed Wilkinson. "No, I'm sure he wouldn't." He stood up slowly. "Can I help in any way?"

"I doubt it. Where can I get in touch with you if something crops up?"

Wilkinson took a card from his pocket and passed it to Gideon.

"Here," he said. "And the children live—"

"I know where they live," Gideon interrupted.

Wilkinson smiled briefly.

"I will tell Entwhistle that you were at least prepared to listen to me," he said. "I won't tell him a word more. Thank you, Commander."

Gideon said dryly, "No need to thank me. I'm only doing my job!"

Wilkinson laughed, as much with satisfaction as because he was amused.

Five minutes later, when Wilkinson had gone, Gideon telephoned Lemaitre, who was in his office although it was lunchtime.

"I was just having a sandwich," he told Gideon. "Then I'm going over myself to have a word with the man who bought the bicycle. He thinks we think he knows it was stolen, but I'll shake him down if I have to. Thanks for ringing, George."

"Keep in touch," Gideon urged.

He himself had a sandwich, spent another quarter of an hour with Hobbs, and then left the office and set out to walk to the Ministry of Power, at Millbank. It was no more than ten minutes away, and he had been cooped up in a car too much today. He crossed the Embankment and walked alongside the river for a hundred yards or so, crossing again by Westminster Bridge, then by the gates of the Houses of Parliament. The Square was a dense mass of red buses; he did not think he had ever seen so many there at one time; obviously there was a traffic holdup in Victoria Street. He passed the Houses of Parliament and strolled alongside the open space near the river. The opposite bank was beginning to take on an almost panoramic skyline. Farther along, beyond Lambeth Bridge, the new Ministry Building looked as if it were made of glass, fragile enough to splinter.

A doorman let him in; a commissionaire took his name. He gave the name of the Minister's personal secretary as the man he wanted to see. Waiting—and wondering how long he would be kept—he let his thoughts go back to the morning and that quite astonishing interview with John Boyd. The further away it became, the more improbable it seemed.

A middle-aged man approached from the lifts.

"Commander Gideon?"

Gideon turned to look at the pale face, the faded gray mustache, the tired gray eyes.

"Mr. Menzies?"

"Yes. Will you please come with me?" They stepped into a lift and the doors closed on them. As he pressed a button, he went on: "The Minister has asked me to apologize that he will have to leave at four o'clock precisely."

That gave them an hour, so he wasn't making light of the visit.

"That should give us plenty of time," Gideon said. At last, he pushed thought of Boyd out of his mind for a few minutes, and concentrated on what he knew of the Minister of Power. The Right Honorable David Wilshire was a relatively young man, being in his late forties. He was also one of the unexpected successes of two administrations. For a man who had a very tricky Ministry to control, with three major nationalized industries within its orbit, it was remarkable that he managed to keep out of public disfavor. Known on television as one who spoke seldom, but always to the point, he was

127

reported to be the only Minister who had ever made the public accept the reasonableness of an increase in the price of coal.

Menzies opened the door of a room which overlooked the Embankment; it was large, with very wide, spacious windows, and as Gideon crossed toward the desk set slantwise across the corner, he realized that this room must have one of the most magnificent views of London. Thought of that faded almost as Wilshire stood up. He was smaller than his television image, very compact, very lean. His face was tanned and stronger than photographs implied; there was something in the set of his lips which gave the impression of strength.

"Good afternoon, Commander. Thank you for coming." Gideon muttered something which sounded vague, even to him. "Do sit down," Wilshire continued. "I think the other chair will be better; it's made for large men!'" Gideon sat down, and found cigarettes and cigars in boxes pushed toward him. "No? It's surprising how many people don't smoke, these days. Yet tobacco sales don't seem to be dropping." The Minister lit a cigarette and leaned back in his chair. "Your concern is with the blackouts we've had recently, I understand."

"It is, sir."

"Sir Reginald made it clear that he is troubled, too."

Gideon hesitated, and then asked gruffly, "Aren't you, sir?"

Wilshire paused, startled at having the ball tossed back so quickly, and then gave a quick, pleasant smile.

"Yes, I am," he admitted.

"Do *you* have reason to suspect sabotage, sir?"

"I hadn't, until I heard from Sir Reginald. I have since consulted some of my advisers, who agree that it could be sabotage. They also believe that it could be coincidence. Nothing is yet conclusive—or have you any sensational revelations to make, Commander?"

Gideon wasn't sure whether he was being gently and cleverly taken down a peg or two, but he had adjusted himself now, and knew exactly what tactics to adopt: bluff forthrightness, no beating about the bush, no vacillating.

"No, sir," he said. "I hope there won't be any need for sensational revelations. They could cause too much havoc. Nor have I any positive evidence that there is a connection between the instances of damage, but that some are sabotage there is no doubt at all. It is my considered view that these breakdowns may be organized by the same group of people, and obviously they could become more frequent and more serious. With winter coming on, we don't want to lose any time."

"If you are right, we certainly don't."

"We don't even if I'm wrong," Gideon said. "We don't want the possibility hanging over our heads, and we at the Yard are too busy with the more common forms of crime to want to spend unnecessary time on this." He wondered if he was being too blunt; if he was slipping into aggressiveness. "All our resources are stretched to breaking point, sir—like all government departments, I suppose."

Wilshire looked at him speculatively, no longer with a half smile. Gideon thought, He has a lot of power—can he use it properly? He did not feel anxious for himself, was concerned only for what might happen.

Then Wilshire put out his cigarette, and asked, "What exactly do you want from me?"

"Authority to investigate all the cases we suspect of being sabotage."

"With or without the cooperation of our security officers?"

"I would like them instructed to cooperate."

"Do you doubt their readiness to do so?"

"I doubt their readiness to believe that some of the incidents are sabotage," Gideon said. "And I don't think they're the only people in the nationalized and other industries who would doubt it."

"You seem *very* sure, Commander."

"I am very sure that every case should be treated as sabotage until we've proved that it isn't," Gideon said.

"If it is so treated, don't you think your attitude might be regarded as alarmist?"

Gideon hesitated, and then, without realizing it, he did exactly what Josiah Wilkinson had done in his office. He gripped the arms of his chair and eased himself forward, as if about to get up. He sensed a certain disapproval in Wilshire's expression, even derision.

"I'm alarmed already, sir," Gideon said. "I'm sorry I've wasted your time."

He knew, as he said it, that he was asking for trouble. And he knew also that he was dabbling in politics and spheres of influence which were none of his business and often beyond his understanding. But it was said, and he did not regret it. He had a mental picture of John Boyd, and compared the two men, each the antithesis of the other, and he did not know which one he mistrusted more. When Wilshire made no move, he stood up.

He had no idea what a towering and impressive figure he made; no idea of the impression he was making on the Minister, who sat back without change of expression and stared up. Slowly Gideon backed away, pushing the chair aside. There seemed nothing to say but "Good afternoon, sir."

"If you had your guess," asked Wilshire, "what would you say is the motive? Political, industrial, or criminal, in the sense that someone wants to cash in?"

What was he saying? That he accepted the theory of a campaign of sabotage? Gideon deliberated, and then answered gruffly, "I'd say that the main probability is a criminal motivation."

"That would be a considerable relief," remarked the Minister. "Have you any reason for saying that?" He motioned to Gideon's chair, casually.

Gideon sat down again, as casually.

130

"It is only a guess," he admitted.

"You mean you find an industrial or a political motive hard to believe?"

"That about sums it up, sir."

"A lot of the industrial security men find organized sabotage itself hard to believe."

"That shouldn't prevent them acting on the possibility," argued Gideon. "We would go all out to find the men involved whether we knew they were doing it for political, industrial, or criminal motives. I mean criminal in your sense, of course."

"I think we understand each other," Wilshire said dryly. "Have you any idea how long it will take you to find the truth?"

"No, sir, not the slightest. It could be months. It might be days. It really depends on whether we have another breakdown in the near future or not—and whether at the time of such a breakdown we have full security established at all power, transmission, and transformer stations."

To his astonishment, Wilshire actually laughed.

"In other words, if there's another power failure and we can't trace the cause or the culprit, it will be my fault. I certainly can't risk that! I've arranged for representatives of the three nationalized industries concerned—electricity, gas, and coal—to meet you when we've finished."

He pressed a bell by the side of his desk and went on, "I'm glad you're not a politician, Commander! Now let's have some tea."

Carol Entwhistle sat at the tea table, but did not eat.

Florence Entwhistle, her aunt, a graying woman no longer young, looked at her anxiously, but said nothing. It would do no good, and would only drive the child into one of her long silences. The one thing she knew that Carol enjoyed was helping in the garden, and after tea, when the others had gone, she went into the back garden of the pleasant house on the new estate, and began to clip the edges of the grass with a small pair of hand shears. After five minutes, Carol emerged. Her aunt appeared not to notice her. Carol sauntered over, looking downcast as always, and stood close by. Normally she would pick up one of the tools, and dig or rake the grass. Today she stood for a long time doing nothing, until her aunt felt that the growing tension was enough to make her scream.

Suddenly, Carol spoke.

"Auntie."

Thank God!

"Yes, Carol?"

"What is it like to be dead?"

Florence looked up, shaken by the question.

"What on earth made you ask that?"

"I want to know."

"Yes, but why do you want to know?"

"That little girl's dead, isn't she?"

"What little— Oh. The one whose picture was in the paper?"

"Yes."

"Yes, she's dead."

"So *she* knows what it's like to be dead, doesn't she?"

The woman, on her knees with a piece of matting to save her stockings, said in a mood of helpless resignation, "Yes, I suppose so."

"And my mummy knows, doesn't she?"

"She—yes, Carol, she knows."

"Then why don't *you* know?"

"Because I—because I'm alive, Carol. I'm not dead."

"My mummy knew what it was like when she was alive," Carol stated.

Florence Entwhistle did not speak, but put the shears down and got to her feet. This was a moment which came so rarely. Carol was talking without being cajoled or persuaded, and her aunt did not know how best to cope.

Only an hour before, she had talked to Josiah Wilkinson, who had urged her to do everything she possibly could to make the child talk about her mother, but now the opportunity was here she did not know how to use it.

Slowly she said, "I don't think she did, Carol."

The child nodded in agreement with her own assertion.

"How do you know that?" asked Florence.

"Because she told me so," answered Carol simply.

"*Did* she?" asked her aunt, and she realized that she was doing the right thing—by being skeptical she was making Carol try to prove that she was right. "I think she must have been teasing you."

"No, she wasn't teasing," Carol insisted.

"How do you know she wasn't?"

"Because she was crying," Carol said, "and she only teased when she was laughing."

Florence looked down at the pale face so full of promise for the future. She prayed for guidance, sensing that Carol might now talk of those things buried deep in her mind, things that might well be the reason for her withdrawal from the world into herself. Seldom had the blue eyes stared up so straight and with such confidence.

"So she must have known what it was like to be dead," she reasoned simply.

God, God, tell me the right thing to say!

"Did she tell *you* what it was like, Carol?"

"She didn't exactly *tell* me."

"What did she say?"

"She said living alone was awful; it was like being dead."

"Oh," said Florence. Dear God help me. "I know what she meant; it *is* awful to be on your own all the time."

"How do you know, Auntie? *You've* got Uncle Dick."

"I didn't always have Uncle Dick, and once he had to go away for a long time. So I was on my own then."

"*Was* it like being dead?" asked Carol.

She mustn't lie, mustn't foster this strange delusion, and

yet she must not spoil the child's faith in her mother. If only Josiah Wilkinson were here!

"Sometimes I *thought* it was," she said huskily.

"You didn't know, like my mummy?"

"No, Carol, not for certain. How—how often did Mummy talk to you like this?"

"Not very often," Carol answered reflectively. "But she said I was the only one she could talk to about it, because I could understand."

No, that couldn't be true; Margaret must have meant something different from that, Florence thought. But it wouldn't do to argue too much with the child now; it might drive her back into herself. There must be a way of making her tell more, of keeping this newly given confidence.

"And could you understand?" asked Florence.

"I must have, because Mummy said I could."

Almost in anguish, Florence asked herself what she should say next, and through the silence while she tried to make up her mind, she heard Clive's voice from some distance off. Other voices sounded; obviously he was with a crowd of boys, but he would soon be here and he would break the spell. In one way she hated that, in another she was glad, for it relieved her of the agony of deciding what to say.

She saw a change come over Carol's expression, and suddenly Carol looked downward, hiding her eyes, holding her hands in front of her, the fingers interlocked. Then, when Clive's voice sounded nearer, she looked up at her aunt with a penetrating, pleading gaze.

"Don't tell Clive," she begged. "Don't tell Clive. He only laughs at me!"

"I won't tell Clive," Florence assured her quietly. "I promise."

The child held her gaze for a few seconds, then dropped it. Clive shouted to someone unseen, "After supper, then," and came running from the front gate, long-limbed, tall for his age, outwardly thoroughly happy. "Auntie, can I go to Jim-

134

my's after supper—he's going to have a lot of fellows in."

"You can go if you get your homework done first."

"Oh, great! I'll go and do it now." Clive turned and rushed away, pulling his sister's hair as he went. She did not protest; she did not even look up as he disappeared into the house.

16 *The Fathers*

George Jensen senior was a good man, according to his lights. There was some narrow-mindedness in him, and bigotry, but in other ways there was tolerance and understanding. He was strict with his children, and for that matter with his wife, but he was also kind and generous. He was a shop steward at a factory in Bethnal Green—not far from Mickle & Stratton—and he was a lay preacher and a steward at the local Methodist church. He was a small, thin-featured man, and no one who had ever seen him side by side with his son could doubt their relationship.

His wife knew and understood him well.

She was a much shrewder woman than she appeared to be, with her frequent, high-pitched laugh and her comeliness and her apparent lack of interest in anything except gossip and her family. Because her husband was strict, she was inclined to be lenient—but never, as far as she knew, overindulgent.

Both of them had been troubled by their second son, George junior, for some time. It was not simply because he did not join in church and youth-club activities with the eagerness he had shown at one time: it was the fact that he had become more and more uncommunicative.

"Where are you off to, Georgie?" his mother would say.

"Out."

"Where's out?"

"In the great open spaces beyond the front door!"

"Don't you talk to me like that, young man, or I'll let you know who's master here!"

But his mother never did—for he *was* eighteen years old.

"George."

"Yes, Father."

"Why weren't you at the Social Club dance?"

"I was somewhere else that night—things clashed, see."

"Who were you out with?"

"Friends."

"What friends, my son?"

"You wouldn't know them, Dad."

But, in fact, his father did know them—or, at least, know of them. He had neighbors with children of their own, and friends at church and work, and by casual questioning he learned that George was often with a group of high-spending youths who gambled far too much. Most of their gambling was with the East End firm of Jackie Spratt's Limited, and in the beginning George Jensen senior had thought it would be only a matter of time before his son got into debt and would come to him for help. *That* would be the time to remonstrate and reason with him.

It did not happen; indeed, his son appeared to have more, rather than less, money to spend. True, he did not waste it, but spent it on clothes and was saving up for a Continental holiday, but George senior could not understand how he came by it. Most punters were in debt very early in their gambling; very few had more than a few lucky winners before coming a cropper. He knew there were "systems" and he knew that some men developed successful systems for a time, but they invariably failed in the long run. And his son had no knowledge of racing, no special source of information. Why, one of the men at work was the brother of a famous jockey and even *he* could never be sure of backing a winner!

How was it that George did?

Jensen senior asked Ted Smith, the foreman carpenter to whom George was apprenticed, as they walked home from church one Sunday morning.

"I can't understand it either, George. He's always got money, lends quite a bit to some of the others—even older

137

men who ought to know better than to borrow from a kid. But he never talks about it much. I know one thing."

"What's that?"

"He goes to the Mill Lane betting shop, not the one near you."

So George the father made a point of finding out where the Mill Lane office was—and discovered it, with the chemical factory behind and, in the distance, the mass of London's docks. He did not go there often, and did not follow his son, but he made discreet inquiries until one day he had what he believed to be a stroke of luck; he found out that one of the fitters at work lived in Mill Lane, nearly opposite the betting shop .

When his son did not come home on the evening following the fire at Mickle & Stratton, George Jensen senior went to see this workmate, a man named Mills. The family Mills of Mill Lane had been in the same little house for three generations. There was still a grandfather, in his nineties, who had the top front room and whose eyesight was as keen, he claimed, as it had been when he was a boy.

"Ain't no doubt about it," he told Jensen in his frail brittle voice. "I see your George, Mr. Jensen—spit image of you when you was a boy, he is. I see him go in but I never see him go out. Left his bike outside he did, didn't trouble to lock it. Someone else come along and took it. You can't trust no one these days."

Jensen was sure that the old man's story was true.

He also knew that the police had been making inquiries about his son.

What he did not know, but his wife did, was that George had come home late the previous night, changed his clothes, and gone out again. His bedroom had smelled faintly of burning, as if something had been singed, and there were fragments of wood shavings left by his shoes.

"It's nobody's business but my boy's," Mrs. Jensen had told herself as she cleaned the room.

138

She slept; while her husband lay wakefully beside her, listening to her loud breathing, to the sound of distant traffic, to the thumping of his own heart.

"I must give the boy a chance," he kept telling himself over and over again. "I must try to help him."

At last he, too, fell asleep.

Next morning, he left at half past seven to cycle to work as usual, but he did not go straight to the factory. Once there, he would not be able to get time off. He cycled to the docks and watched the work going on in the Pool of London, and just after ten o'clock he went to Jackie Spratt's Betting Shop in Mill Lane.

"There's an old geezer here says he knows young Jensen came here the day before yesterday," a man told the stocks and shares office manager, to whom George Jensen had gone for help. "My God, what are we going to do?"

"We don't get into a panic," the manager said. "Stand by, Biddle, and leave this to me."

The manager's name was Rupert Kano, and he was in his shirt sleeves when he went into his office and saw old Jensen. He concealed the shock of surprise at seeing a man so like the boy who was dead, and said with brisk certainty, "You must be mistaken, sir. No one named Jensen is on the books, and certainly no one of that name was here on Monday."

George Jensen knew beyond all doubt that this was a lie. He stood staring, heart beating fast, not sure what to do. If he simply said he was sorry and left, he could go straight to the police—*they* would make the man tell the truth. But the truth might do grave harm to his son, and he had to do everything he possibly could for the boy.

"That's a lie," he said quietly. "And I can prove it."

"You can't prove what isn't true," Rupert Kano retorted. "What makes you think you can prove it?"

"Because he was seen coming here on his bicycle—and

someone was seen stealing the bicycle," George Jensen said stiffly. "I don't know what influence you have over my son or what you are doing with him, but I want to know where he is. And I'm not going to be put off with any lies."

The shirt-sleeved man said smoothly, "I'm sure it's a mistake, Mr. Jensen, but there's just one possibility. My assistant who was on duty on Monday afternoon won't be in for an hour. As soon as he arrives, I'll speak to him. He may know something. Can you be back here in an hour and a half, say?"

Something like elation filled Jensen, but he did not show any sign of it as he said sternly, "I want to know where my son is." And then, to make his point absolutely clear, he told one of the few lies he had ever told in his life. "I saw him come in here—I *know* he was here."

"Then my colleague may be able to help," said Rupert Kano.

When Jensen had gone, Kano sent for Biddle, and said, "The old man's been spying on his son. He'll be back in an hour and a half—if nothing happens to him on the way. Fix him."

"It's not so easy," Biddle began.

"I didn't say it was easy," Rupert Kano said. "I said fix him."

As George Jensen cycled away from Mill Lane, passing a lorryload of sulfuric acid being driven from the factory behind the bookmaker's, Geoffrey Entwhistle was shifting books on the shelves of the prison library at Dartmoor, while another convict, a self-confessed murderer, was dusting the shelves. Entwhistle was obsessed by thoughts of his children. He had left them voluntarily for three years, but then Margaret had been with them; now he hated the thought that they were growing up without him.

He finished the job, and then reported to the warder in charge that he was through.

140

"Do it again," the warder said.

There was a break for a meal in the canteen—reasonable food in the hateful hall beneath the hateful watch kept by armed men. It was the daily routine: a low-pitched rumble of talk, the clattering of knives and forks and plates, the usual complaints for the sake of being able to utter some words freely, then straight back to the library.

The first person he saw was Josiah Wilkinson, and for a moment his heart seemed to stand still.

"We can talk over here," Wilkinson said quietly. "We have permission." He led the way to a corner where there was a table spread with old, dog-eared magazines. "I saw the children," he added. "They're all extremely well."

Entwhistle dropped heavily into a chair; he was sweating from reaction, and could not find words.

"I also saw Commander Gideon," Wilkinson went on. "And he listened."

"Listened," echoed Entwhistle hoarsely. Then he muttered, "Will he *do* anything? That's what matters."

"He has promised to review the investigation," answered Wilkinson, "but it doesn't really mean anything unless we can give him something to work on. If we can, he will do all he can."

Entwhistle said with an effort, "Well, I suppose it's something. Better than a flat 'no.' How—how is Carol?"

"When I saw her, much the same," answered Wilkinson, "but when I got home last night—very late—I had a telephone call about her from your sister-in-law."

Entwhistle sat very tense.

"Carol's beginning to talk about her mother," went on Wilkinson. "That can only be a good thing."

When his visitor left the library, Entwhistle sat in absolute stillness. The warder who had been so indifferent in the morning saw him, studied the expression on his face, the strange look that was almost of hope and yet had the mark of despair on it. The warder could have stirred him and sent him back to work on the books. Instead, he left him alone.

Entwhistle *did* feel hope; but he had become so accustomed to the death of hope that it was almost an emotion of fear.

Old Jeff Mickle forced his way out of the ancient Rolls-Royce and squeezed himself through the doorway of the new "factory." Inside, twenty or thirty men were working, a new circular saw was being bolted to the cement floor, while stocks of wood were being carried in. Tony, his son, had taken off his jacket and was hot and perspiring as he helped in the work and talked to two men, one of them the foreman carpenter Ted Smith. Old Jeff, sweating freely, looking like a bloated John Bull, his enormous clothes a lot too tight for him, watched his son with warm approval.

But as he reached him, he bellowed, "Hey! What's holding you back, Tony boy? We want to get this place working, didn't I tell you! We've got the orders—you know what? We've got the contract for that new hotel in Bournemouth. Remember it's Mickle & Son now—just Mickle & Son!"

The remarkable thing was that the men began to work harder.

Gideon reached the office that morning, wasted no time over his briefing, then sent for Hobbs to discuss the powerhouse investigation. Waiting for Hobbs, he discovered that he had left his notes about the sabotage at home. He had been under such pressure for the past day or two that he welcomed a brief respite, and decided to go back to get them himself. He turned in to the gateway of his house, and heard the piano being played with a joyous zest which broke through his preoccupation with the day's events and brought a smile to his lips. He recognized the piece but could not place it. Tchaikovsky—that was it—the "Nutcracker" suite! Remembering the name was a triumph for Gideon. It was one of Penelope's favorites, and she played it whenever she was happy. Greatly cheered, he opened the front door—and saw Kate near the front-room door, listening but looking toward him. She raised a hand to stop him from speaking. He closed the door with hardly a sound. The sound of music filled the house and gave it a brightness that was near radiance. He stepped to Kate's side and slid his arm around her waist. She took his hand, twining her fingers through his. There was a glow in her eyes as she listened to her child playing with such triumph.

At last, Penelope stopped.

Her back was to the door and the baby grand, a Bechstein, was slantwise across the corner, in a similar position to the Right Honorable David Wilshire's desk. Penelope sprang up from the stool, pirouetted toward the window, disappeared from sight—and then exclaimed:

"Daddy!"

She reappeared, eyes glowing, young body childishly appealing in her short, sleeveless dress. She caught him in a dramatic hug, then stood back.

"I haven't told him," Kate said.

"Daddy," his daughter said eagerly, earnestly, "Jonathan's asked me to marry him. And I do love him. I truly do."

All Gideon could think of was the radiance in his daughter's face and a vague mental picture of a pleasant youth who had been in and out of the house for the past few months. But if Jonathan had been an ogre, Gideon couldn't have said so to Penelope now.

17 *The "Accident"*

George Jensen stood on Tower Hill and stared at the flow of people going into the Tower. Two beefeaters were on duty near the gates, while the guards marched up and down with their endless military precision. A few people were sitting or standing idly about Tower Hill, too old or too indolent for work. The Tower itself stood ageless. Down in the grassy moat, a few soldiers kicked a football in a desultory, time-wasting way.

George had always loved this part of London.

Behind him was the high building of the Port of London Authority, to his right the narrow street leading to Eastcheap and Mincing Lane, to Billingsgate Market and to the Monument. As a boy, he had worked here, and weekends when he was on his own he would often return, staying most of the day.

It was nearly half past eleven—time to go back to Mill Lane.

He unlocked the safety chain of his bicycle, which was parked close to the curb, and cycled off with his slow, deliberate movements. He knew the City and the East End well enough to be able to keep pace with the new one-way turnings, and although he could go up to Aldgate and then to Whitechapel, the quickest way was to cycle past the forbidding walls of the Mint, then toward Wapping High Street with the dark warehouse walls on one side, and then to walk his bicycle through the alleys until he was at the bottom end of Mill Lane, close to the chemical factory.

He did not realize that he had been followed by two men.

The first man was Biddle from Jackie Spratt's, who was at the wheel of a dilapidated van. The other was Detective Sergeant Leslie Bell of N.E. Division, in a utility van driven by an older detective officer.

There was a thick buildup of traffic at a junction near the Mint, and Jensen was able to get through more quickly on his bicycle than either of the two vehicles. The stench of diesel exhaust and the grating roar of powerful engines were all around him.

"We're going to lose him," Detective Sergeant Bell said. "I'll nip out—I may be able to keep up." He climbed out of the van as traffic began to move again, and strode after Jensen.

At the same time, Biddle thought, He's going the back way.

Biddle began to fret and fume, then saw a gap in the traffic through which he could squeeze, drove to Aldgate, and then turned in to Whitechapel Road, approaching Mill Lane from the top end. He did not drive down Mill Lane but along another, parallel road, and reached the bottom end as George Jensen came out of a cobbled alley and straddled his bicycle. Biddle knew that someone else was in the alley, but took no notice. Jensen was within a minute of reaching the office again, and he mustn't get there.

Biddle was sweating.

He swung the wheel of the van when he was only ten yards behind Jensen, who heard the rasping of tires on the graveled road and turned his head in alarm. He saw the van bearing down on him but had no chance to change direction or to dodge.

At that instant, P.C. Race, who had been sent to watch Jackie Spratt's shop, saw what was happening. Without a moment's hesitation, virtually without thought, he leapt forward in an effort to push the cyclist out of the way. He might have succeeded but for an instinctive action on the older

145

man's part, for Jensen flung himself to one side, trying to clear the crossbar of his bicycle.

He failed.

Race might have saved him had he stayed on his bicycle, but as it was he hardly had time to save himself.

Jensen crashed down, and the van struck him. His head smashed against the curb, and he knew a fraction of a second of intense pain before losing consciousness. Biddle jammed on his brakes and sat shivering in his seat. Two men and several women, approaching, stopped in their tracks and stared with horror. A man farther away came running and another appeared from behind the old van. Race got up, bruised and grazed, and then went down on one knee beside the cyclist.

There was blood everywhere, all over the forehead and the face—everywhere.

The running man drew up.

"My God!" he exclaimed. And then hoarsely: "We need an ambulance."

Detective Sergeant Leslie Bell took a tiny two-way radio from his inside pocket, called his station, and reported.

"There's been an accident between a van and a bicycle in Mill Lane. Doctor and ambulance are needed urgently. This is Detective Sergeant Bell," he added hastily. "I will wait at the scene of the accident until both arrive."

He switched off, glanced at Race, and said, "Bloody good try; I'll see the Superintendent hears about this," then stared coldly at Biddle, who was watching him openmouthed.

"Come down out of there," he ordered.

"I—I didn't see him!" Biddle cried. "He came out of nowhere!"

"You saw him," Bell said. "Get down, and answer some questions."

"I—I—I didn't see him!" Biddle insisted. He climbed down slowly, lips quivering, teeth chattering. Others came up

146

now, mesmerized by the crushed, bloodied body, the wrecked bicycle, the shaking driver.

"He drove straight at him," a woman said accusingly.

"I didn't—I didn't see him!"

"What's your name?"

"Biddle, John Biddle, I—"

"Let me see your license," Bell said stonily.

Slowly, Biddle took out his wallet. More and more people gathered around, until there was quite a crowd when the ambulance arrived, its bell ringing, followed by more police. The drab street was suddenly crowded and noisy. Police pushed their way through to the injured man, and a young doctor followed. Bell, writing down the details from the license, watched both the driver's face and the doctor's.

"He's alive," the doctor stated. "That's about all I can say for him."

"I didn't see him!" said Biddle shrilly.

"You must have seen him," said Race. "You didn't give him a chance."

Oddly, the words did not seem ironic to him; they were literally true.

Two telephones rang on Rupert Kano's desk at the same time. He lifted them with both hands, said "Just a moment" into one and "Kano here" into the other.

A man spoke in a very quiet, almost whispering voice.

"They're tightening security everywhere, Rupe."

Kano put a hand over the mouthpiece of the other telephone and said, "What do you mean?"

"I told you Gideon had been out to New Bridge, didn't I?"

"Yes."

"Since then, security's been tightened at all the power stations, not just one or two. And Gideon was at the Ministry yesterday."

"All right," said Kano. "I get you."

"You won't fix any more blackouts, will you?"

"Not until I know what's going on," said Kano.

He rang off without another word, held the mouthpiece of the second telephone tightly, and stared out of the tiny window. He opened his lips and tapped his teeth, which were very white, with his fingernail. Then, slowly, he put the other telephone to his mouth.

"Sorry to keep you," he said.

"Mr. Kano, they look as if they're going to take Biddle to the police station," a man said excitedly. "I was upstairs—I saw it happen! He knocked a man off a bicycle; it looks as if he killed him."

"Does it," Rupert Kano said coldly. "He never could drive."

He put the second receiver down, stood up, stepped to the door, and put on his jacket. Without saying a word to anybody, he went through the betting shop and into the street. The crowd was still thick at the far end of the lane, and an ambulance was coming his way. Beyond were several policemen, Biddle's van, and two cars.

Rupert Kano walked toward the Mile End Road.

He was a compact, athletic figure, with his bow tie, dark curly hair, highly polished shoes, and brisk walk. Without once looking around, he reached the main street and, a few minutes later, went into Aldgate East Station. He took a District Line train as far as Charing Cross, and from there walked toward Buckingham Street and Adelphi. He went into a small block of new flats, and a lift took him up to the penthouse. He stepped into the main bedroom, which overlooked the river, and stripped down to his underpants. He went into the big, modern bathroom, ran water first into a handbasin, then into a bath. He took a lotion from a cabinet, poured it into the handbasin, and began to wash his hair.

Almost at once the water was stained black.

He emptied the basin and washed again and again with the same shampoo, then studied himself in the mirror. It was difficult to recognize in the fair-haired man the one who had entered the room a short while before. Even his eyelashes had changed color. He finished off with a bath, then toweled himself vigorously. He put on a dressing gown and went into the living room, which also overlooked the river. He sat back in an easy chair and dialed a City number.

A woman answered.

"This is Sir Geoffrey Craven's secretary."

"This is Wilcox," Kano said.

"Just a moment, Mr. Wilcox." The moment proved a long one, but Rupert Kano alias Wilcox did not move.

At last, a man spoke in a pleasant, cultured voice.

"Is this a true emergency?"

"Yes," Wilcox said flatly.

"If it is about the security precautions at—" began Sir Geoffrey Craven.

"It's more than that," said Wilcox.

"Where are you?"

"In Johns Street."

"I'll see you in an hour, but I won't have long," Craven said brusquely.

"If we're not careful, *we* won't have long," said Wilcox. He put the receiver down as abruptly as he had in Mill Lane, and went into the bedroom. He put on a pale fawn-colored suit of a noticeably different cut from the one he had been wearing, then went into the kitchen and plugged in a kettle. He made himself some coffee, drank it black, and left the flat immediately afterward. Fifty-five minutes from the time he had put down the telephone, he entered an office building near the Bank of England, and was taken up in a hand-operated lift to the fifth floor. On the door leading to the offices was the name "Sir Geoffrey Craven & Co., Ltd.— Merchant Bankers." There were also a number of other registered company offices. Among them were "Hibild, Ltd.," "Associated Euro-Electronics, Ltd.," and "Hotel Fitted Furniture Suppliers, Ltd."

149

Kano alias Wilcox went in, and pressed a bell marked "Inquiries." A young woman in a short sheath dress above very long legs came toward him.

"Good morning, Mr. Wilcox."

"Good morning, Sylvia."

"Sir Geoffrey is expecting you." The girl led the way along a narrow passage to the big room in which Craven was sitting. He was tall and very thin, with hawk-like features and a deeply lined face. Wilcox, obviously at ease, obviously on equal terms with this man, shook hands.

"What is it?" Craven asked.

"I've had to leave Mill Lane," Wilcox announced.

"It had to happen sooner or later," Craven said. "Is it such an emergency?"

"I think one of our men, Biddle, will tell the police about young Jensen and the fire," said Wilcox. "And Stratton, who would have sold out to us, tells me he's been slung out of Easiphit. Old Mickle won't give in. I think we ought to withdraw our offer at once."

Craven nodded.

"I've always treated the Mill Lane office as a dead end—somewhere to walk out of one day, and now I'm out," Wilcox said. "But the police will probably try to discover if there is a working arrangement between me and Jackie Spratt's. As Kano, I had the Board of Trade license for dealing in stocks and shares, but he put up the money."

"Can they prove it?"

"No. But they may suspect it strongly enough to start at the top," said Wilcox. "Gideon is an old friend of Lemaitre, and they work closely together." He paused, only to go on: "And Gideon was at the Ministry of Power yesterday *and* at New Bridge."

"So I am informed," said Craven.

Neither of the men spoke for a few minutes, and it was Craven who broke the silence: "Gideon *is* only a policeman."

"He's a policeman who makes one visit to the Ministry of

Power, and within hours the whole security of the power stations is doubled, in some cases trebled," retorted Wilcox.

After a pause, Craven asked, "What is it you want to do?"

"I think we should act at once," said Wilcox. "If we don't, we may not be able to act at all. If the police do trace a connection between Spratt and the fires, we may find them uncomfortably close to us, and we would have to stop everything. I don't think we can afford to wait."

After another, longer pause, Craven said, "You couldn't possibly mean that *you* can't wait, could you?"

"No," said Wilcox. "I could leave England today and live in luxury for the rest of my life; you know that very well. By staying even an extra three or four days, I'm taking a risk. But I want Electronics New Age."

"Is it really worth the risk?" asked Craven. "We could wait a few weeks—a few months, even—until this scare blows over. We're not really pushed yet. You've always gone in and out of the country under your real name of Wilcox; nothing need prevent you from going out and coming back when the time is more propitious. I think there's an unnecessary risk of failure if we strike now."

"I don't," Wilcox replied. "If I know Gideon, and I've made a study of the way he works, he will anticipate what we're planning. He's done it twice before, to my knowledge —divined a plot, I mean, simply from his knowledge of the circumstances. He may have plumped for the sabotage-for-its-own-sake theory, but he won't neglect anything else. Give him a week or two, and he'll have worked out a scheme to block whatever we do. If we stop after we've got Electronics New Age, then we're home and dry. We'll have everything we need; we needn't push firms like Easiphit, and with Jensen dead that can't be traced to us. Hibild is as safe as houses at the moment. Once we've stopped operating, Gideon will never get us. If we simply postpone this job, we'll lose Electronics New Age, but if we lie low and start work on something else in a few weeks or a few months, the police may be waiting to pounce. In any case—I doubt if *Boyd* can wait."

"That's the most convincing thing you've said yet," remarked Craven. "All right, we'd better meet somewhere tonight."

"Not somewhere," Wilcox corrected. "My place. Let's say ten o'clock."

Craven did not argue.

18 *Hobbs*

Deputy Commander Alec Hobbs did not know why, but he knew that when Gideon returned from Fulham with his notes about the electricity failures, he was in a much brighter mood. Something at home had pleased him. Hobbs had spent the past few hours going over the cases which had come up during his own absence, and as he studied Gideon's notes, he reflected more than he had ever done on Gideon as a man and as a policeman. Gideon had a gift—which might in fact be an acquired habit—of putting himself into other people's shoes. He could feel deeply for such a man as Entwhistle, for instance, and imagine what Entwhistle would feel like if he was actually innocent. He could suffer with Frank Morrison and at the same time sympathize with, and so understand, Lillian Morrison in her distress.

In some ways, this characteristic had disadvantages. For all his stern exterior, Hobbs thought, Gideon was perhaps too softhearted. But it had one enormous advantage. He could put himself into a criminal's shoes and think like him, working out what the criminal was likely to do, and thus could anticipate it. A surprising number of men and women were in jail because of this quality in Gideon. The most remarkable fact to Hobbs, however, was that Gideon was not wholly aware of the quality. It worked mostly through his subconscious.

And Hobbs believed that Gideon's preoccupation with Entwhistle, for instance, often busied his subconscious mind

153

while his conscious one was dealing with a larger-scale case, like that of the sabotage.

Some time that afternoon, Gideon would send for him, and he checked with the Superintendents, including Lemaitre, so that he would be able to give Gideon the latest information about them all.

He could not tell Gideon about Lillian Morrison, however.

She stood in front of the dressing-table mirror in her home, staring not at her reflection but at a photograph. It was of Frank and Sheila, taken the year before. She, Lillian, had been at the window, watching them playing in the garden, Sheila running, Frank catching and lifting her high. Lillian had rushed downstairs to get the camera, and snapped them. It had been one of those lucky chances, a perfect photograph.

They looked so gloriously happy, as in fact they had been. *She* had been, too; on top of the world.

And Sheila was dead.

Frank was—a murderer.

And it was *her* fault. If she hadn't been tempted into that shop, if her fancy hadn't been taken by the little flower hat, *if, if, if, if . . .*

She stood up slowly.

She stood at the window looking down on the spot where they had been standing for the picture. Two gardens along, a neighbor waved, but she did not respond. She went slowly downstairs and along to the kitchen, knowing exactly what she was going to do. She had no doubt that Frank hated her, blaming her for Sheila's death. There had been times of tension because she could have no more children—he had blamed her for that, too.

And he was right; she had never told him that she took birth-control pills. He didn't dream that was the explanation of her "barrenness." She closed the kitchen door. Frank had fitted a patent sealing strip, to keep out drafts, both at this and at the back door. She drew the curtains across the window, so that no one could see in, then put a cushion down close to the gas stove, opened the oven door, turned on the tap, and put her head inside.

She could smell the gas.

Soon she would be unconscious.

She did not feel any fear or distress, just relief, as sleep stole over her.

Gideon finished the final draft for the power-cuts investigation and pressed the bell for Hobbs, who as usual came in quickly but without any show of haste.

Gideon motioned to a chair, asking, "Anything more from Lemaitre since Jensen senior was injured?"

"No. The driver, Biddle, hasn't admitted anything yet. Neither has Kano turned up. According to the manager of the betting shop, Kano simply had an office there."

"Could it be true?"

"It isn't likely. Lemaitre is checking."

"How's the old chap?"

"Hanging on," said Hobbs.

"Anything we can do for the wife?" asked Gideon.

"She's at the bedside, and we've a man there, too."

Gideon nodded.

"Epping?"

"Nothing."

"Piluski?"

"Wants to see you about six o'clock."

"You stay, too, will you?"

"Yes."

"Now," said Gideon, with the air of a man who had cleared away all the obstacles to a real problem. "The power cuts. Did you study Piluski's report on our visit to the New Bridge Power Station?"

"Yes. It's a first-class report."

"How does the man Boyd show up in it?"

"Almost a dangerous fanatic—I would say extreme right-wing, politically, from his general comments."

"Yes," said Gideon. "Yes. That's how he came through to me."

"Aren't you convinced?"

"Something worries me," said Gideon. "I don't know what it is. The penny will drop, eventually. Now! If it *is* sabotage with a view to causing damage to industry, or on political grounds, we can't do much more. All the security men are doing what they're told—"

Hobbs interrupted.

"I forgot a note from Piluski."

"What is it?"

"Every power station in the Greater London area now has special guards, and we've a man in each station for every shift. There is also a direct line from every station to our nearest Divisional office. He had no trouble, simply followed your instructions."

"Good," said Gideon, obviously thinking about what he was going to say next. "But what if it isn't sabotage for the sake of it? What if it's much simpler—a plot to cause chaos at some key period so that a major series of robberies can be staged?"

"You favor that theory, don't you?" said Hobbs.

"I suppose I really want it to be that; it's a kind of wishful thinking," said Gideon. "I've made some notes of possibilities." He pushed them across. "It seems to me that banks, post offices, and jewelers' shops would be the obvious targets —not necessarily all three. If I were planning such a coup, I would want at least four things. The men to make the raids. Transport to get the stuff away. A distribution center or centers from which to send the booty out. And a final destination, where the stolen goods would be bought or cached."

Hobbs said, "You make out a pretty sound hypothetical case."

"Missed something, I expect," Gideon said. "But we can fill in the gaps. Now—jewelry. Small stuff, easy to take, and fairly easy to hide, but loses its value whenever it's sold. Customs are very hot these days; the first thing we would do obviously is to alert them, so the stolen goods would have to be stored in England for some time unless a charter plane was standing ready. So—see my note—we need a comprehensive nationwide check on all charter and privately owned planes."

Hobbs nodded.

"Not easy, but it can be done, and we might catch other fish in the net," said Gideon. "If it's to be raids on post offices or banks—then the loot will probably be in banknotes."

Again Hobbs nodded.

"Not much of a market overseas, certainly not in big quantities," said Gideon. "We know that a lot of the Great Train Robbery currency notes are still stacked away somewhere—they haven't turned up at any bank or clearinghouse. So if banknotes, they would probably be released in *this* country. That's where I would spend mine if I had the choice."

"Yes," said Hobbs.

"Now, no one is going to arrange a blackout to cover a whole area or district to rob one bank or post office. We can take it for granted that it would be on a big scale. How would you do it?"

"Cover as wide an area as possible as quickly as possible," Hobbs answered.

"I'm not sure that I would do it that way," mused Gideon. "I think I would stagger the breakdowns. Think of the size of London. Forty-eight major centers, at least ten banks—probably more—in each. Nearly five hundred banks. Three men for each bank and you would need fifteen hundred men and five hundred cars. Could *you* select fifteen hundred men you could rely on to raid the specified banks and post offices, do the jobs, escape, and then get the money to an agreed collecting center?"

"Fifteen *hundred,*" Hobbs echoed.

"See what I mean? Now, if there were ten different centers, each blacked out, you could move from center to center with

157

three hundred men, and seventy or eighty cars. That would be manageable, but probably too big. You could select one bank at each center with the smaller number of men and cars, but you would have long distances to travel, and would have to cope with all kinds of obstacles which could get in the way. It would be too massive, too widespread. I see the most likely plan as a concentrated effort with the smallest possible margin of error."

Gideon paused, but Hobbs did not speak. Gideon stood up and began to pace the office.

"Follow me carefully, Alec. We've had these warning blackouts from various parts of London. Obviously there was always a danger that we would realize they were deliberate. So—why rehearse and warn us? It wouldn't be difficult at any time to get a man or two into power stations or at lines carrying electricity to the consumers. Why *warn* us—or warn the authorities?"

Hobbs admitted, "I had wondered."

"I wonder a lot. There seem two possibilities, and neither fits into the theories I've just been advancing. One is that the blackouts do some positive damage each time, or else serve a purpose which the perpetrator wants to achieve. Or else again, it's a kind of blackmail—a 'look what we could do if we tried' kind of thing. That could have either political or commercial motives. We ought to find out just who has suffered from the blackouts—whether any particular firm has branches in all the affected areas. See to it tomorrow, will you?"

"Yes," Hobbs answered.

"Whatever the real rod they've got in pickle for us, one fact is a certainty: that they're trying to get us looking in the wrong place for the wrong thing. If we're stretched to our limit, and the blow falls where we don't expect it—" He broke off, and stood looking out the window. "So someone *could* be trying to make us look in the wrong direction," he went on. "See what I'm driving at?"

158

"In a way," answered Hobbs. "But what could be big enough to be worth it?"

"Don't know yet," admitted Gideon. "There are dozens more possibilities than I've covered, of course. But there's one angle we might try fairly soon. Have you got that report on John Boyd yet?"

"No. Is tomorrow morning soon enough?"

"Have to be, I suppose," Gideon said.

"Boyd," echoed Hobbs reflectively.

"Yes."

"He's gone all out to make us believe it's sabotage for political reasons."

"Yes."

"And you think he could be leading us up the garden?" Hobbs looked as if he were just beginning to realize the significance of what Gideon had been saying.

"Obviously he could be."

"But *why?*"

"He wouldn't be the first extreme right-winger to try to blame left-wingers for something he's done himself. The more I think of Boyd, the more I think he's a fanatic. Now, if he set out to get a security officer's job so as to learn the weaknesses of power stations and the vulnerability of London to sabotage, he would be perfectly placed. He knows London power inside out. He could do terrific harm." Gideon began to pace up and down again. "Especially if sabotage was done *in spite* of security at all the power stations being pushed to its maximum. He would then be able to say 'I told you so' and would have established himself as a man of great discernment. The more so," continued Gideon with unusual vehemence, "if his particular power station was the only one which escaped."

He broke off, staring—almost glaring—at Hobbs, then barked, "Well?"

Hobbs said, "I'll find out whether the report on him is ready."

"Do that," said Gideon. "You made sure that Piluski didn't know I was checking on Boyd, didn't you?"

"Yes." Hobbs hesitated. "Do you suspect Piluski?"

"Not for a moment. I'm just being very careful." Gideon picked up a telephone. "Tell the secretarial pool to send in Miss Sale," he ordered, and put the receiver down.

Hobbs, obviously much more troubled than when he had come in, nodded and went out.

Two minutes later, Sabrina Sale came in, looking her rather spinsterish best. She had on a beautifully cut white silk blouse, buttoned high at the neck, her long, nicely shaped legs in sheer stockings, her feet in not very sensible handmade shoes more than capable of catching Gideon's attention.

After a pleasant word or two, he dictated a dozen letters, and passed her the penciled notes for typing. As she went out, the operator called him. "Mr. Moore of Richmond would like to speak to you, sir."

"Put him through," Gideon said, and on the instant his thoughts shifted from the throbbing roar of a power station to the green pleasance of Wimbledon Common and Richmond Park.

A woman who lived two doors away from the Morrisons sat with some sewing in her hands, but could not settle. She kept seeing Lillian Morrison's face at the window, so pale and set. She had not expected Lillian to be at home by herself; it was thought that she had gone to stay with her mother. She might have left by now, of course.

The neighbor got up and went into the garden. She could see the back of the Morrisons' house, with its wide windows and its well-tended garden, and she stood watching; there was something different about it. Puzzled, she tried to think what it was; something seemed to give the house a shut-in look.

Ah! The kitchen window was closed and the curtains drawn. Well, if Mrs. Morrison had decided to go and stay with her mother, she would be likely to draw the blinds; the sun soon took color out of furniture.

But the upstairs curtains weren't drawn.

"I don't like it," she said aloud. "I don't like poking my nose into other people's affairs either, but I don't like this a bit."

She went into the street and along to the Morrisons' house. There was no car outside; no doors or windows were open, and no curtains drawn. She walked along the crazy-paving path and pushed the door, then rang the bell. There was no answer.

"Is everything all right?" a woman's voice asked.

"Oh!" The worried neighbor spun around and saw the neighbor from the other side, a dark-haired, Italian-looking woman. "I don't know, I'm a bit worried. She was standing at the window just now, looking so strange—and the kitchen curtains are drawn."

They hurried around to the back, tried the door, and banged on the window. Other neighbors began to show an interest but there was no response from the house.

"*I* think we ought to break the door down," the Italian-looking woman said.

"Do less damage breaking the window," said a man who had been attracted by the scene. He bent down, picked up a big stone, poised it and warned "Mind the glass; it might fly," and cracked the stone on the window. It did not break or crack. He banged again; it splintered and a single piece fell out. Gingerly, he pulled at the curtain, and immediately gasped, "Phew! Gas! Send for the police, someone!" He used the curtain to handle the broken glass, then forced the catch, and, holding his breath, climbed in.

"Mrs. Morrison has been taken to hospital with carbon-monoxide poisoning," Moore told Gideon. "She put her head in the gas oven. It's touch and go, the hospital authorities tell me. What's the best thing to do about the husband?"

161

"I'll ask Brixton to let him go out with a warder to see her," Gideon said promptly. "If you don't hear from me, he'll be over soon. Which hospital?"

"Richmond Cottage."

"Right," said Gideon.

There was this woman, at death's door. There was old George Jensen at death's door. There was crime and violence everywhere in London, the consequences of crime and the shadow of crime.

All he could do was fight back.

A tap at his door, and Hobbs came in very briskly.

"I've got part of that report on Boyd's record," he said. "He's been keeping very quiet, but there isn't much doubt that he's very right-wing, politically—has been most of his life."

"I'll have a look," said Gideon, holding out one hand to Hobbs and lifting the telephone with the other.

19 *The Decision*

At ten minutes to ten that evening, Raymond Wilcox alias Rupert Kano opened the door of his flat in the Adelphi to both Boyd and Craven. If he saw any significance in the fact that they had come together, he made no comment. It was an overcast evening, and the lights were on; the window overlooking the river was not curtained, but the other windows were. Cigars, brandy, and liqueurs, balloon glasses and liqueur glasses, were on a low table, and after he had poured brandy for them both, Wilcox went into the kitchen and took a coffee percolator off the stove, set it on a tray with sugar and cream, and carried it in.

Boyd was smoking a cigar; Craven a pipe.

Boyd looked massive and healthy, a little too large for his dinner jacket. Craven, in a business suit, was immaculate.

"And what have you two decided?" Wilcox asked, without any change of manner.

"That you're right," declared Boyd bluffly.

Wilcox's expression changed enough to show both surprise and pleasure.

"What decided the issue?" he asked.

"My interview with the great Gee-Gee Gideon," answered Boyd. "That man is all man and all detective. I've never met anyone who seemed as likely to be able to read my thoughts."

"I hope he didn't."

"I think we should act at once in case he did." Boyd made no fuss at all about admitting the danger. "He's certainly

163

made sure he doesn't take any risks either with me or anyone else. I've never seen the industry's security boys so worked up! We had an afternoon conference, announcing all the plans. Gideon's man Piluski was present and they've sewn it up tight. If we want to cut power in any other London station, we'll have to use bombs."

Wilcox had remained standing during all this. Now he sat down slowly and poured out the coffee.

"Then that's what we'll have to do," he said. "Are you all ready?" He looked at Craven, who was leaning back with his legs stretched out in front of him, casual and elegant and apparently completely at ease.

"Yes. I'm ready."

"And you can buy all the Electronics New Age shares that come on the market?"

"Electronics New Age, and the rest," Craven answered calmly. "I estimate twenty million, and I've the resources to buy and facilities to conceal how many I'm buying."

"Where do you expect prices to fall to?"

"About twenty-five per cent."

"And the profit?"

"Over a two- or three-year period, at least a hundred and fifty per cent, based largely on the E.N.A. patents."

"Immediate profit on the general buying?" asked Wilcox.

"Within forty-eight hours, say—two or three million, possibly more."

Wilcox nodded—and Boyd clapped his hands together with explosive resonance.

"Then *when?*" he demanded.

"Tomorrow," said Wilcox, looking at Craven.

"Yes—tomorrow," Craven agreed.

Wilcox moved from his chair and picked up the brandy decanter, poured a little into his glass, and raised it.

"To the new owners of Electronics New Age," he said.

They sipped, each without showing much expression, although Boyd was obviously at great pains not to reveal his

164

delight. He stood up, awkward and ungainly in the dinner jacket that was too small for him, and began to pace the room.

"Now for the details," he said. "The timing, especially. When it's known that E.N.A. will have to cease producing again for at least a week, their shares will go down like rocks in a river, but when will they reach their lowest?"

"It should be established at about two o'clock," answered Craven. "That will give us sufficient time before the stock market closes, and yet not enough for any recovery. The fall will be quick and heavy, as you say, Wilcox—and we can buy throughout the afternoon and first thing in the morning. By the time it's over, we will have full control of E.N.A. and substantial interest in other electronic companies." He shifted in his chair. "Are you quite sure you can do all that is necessary, Boyd?"

"Don't you worry, I can fix it," Boyd assured him, and at last he exploded into a bellow of a laugh, gave another tremendous clap of his hands, and roared, "I always wanted to be a millionaire!"

That was the time when P.C. Race, who had been on duty for twelve hours, went to bed. He was very tired, bruised and sore where he had grazed himself, but he was asleep almost as soon as he touched the pillow. It was as if his attempt to save George Jensen, the father, had placated the conscience which had been taunting him since he had left old Garratt to be devoured by the flames. And it was the time when Gerald Stratton telephoned the girl Loretta, feeling on top of the world. He was being bought out; he would have a small fortune, and money made the Lorettas of this world get ready for bed. It would be a long time before he worked for his living again. It was the time, also, when Hannah Davis finally screwed up her nerve to go and speak to the Entwhistles about Carol. She was overjoyed to hear that Carol appeared to be coming out of her traumatic condition, and that the Reverend Josiah Wilkinson had taken up her father's case.

165

On the other side of London, old Jensen had died. His widow, so suddenly bereaved, was now filled with alarm for her missing son, and spent a sleepless night. And, not far away from her, the driver who had killed Jensen sat alone in his bed-sitting-room, drinking himself into a stupor. He feared that the police would arrest him at any minute; they hadn't yet, and at heart he knew that this was because they wanted to watch him. But the only contact he had was Kano, who had disappeared.

Gideon woke, the next morning, with a clear head and a deeply satisfying sense of well-being. He had had an early night, being very tired, and could remember dropping off to sleep with Penny's joyous piano-playing in his ears. He was to meet Jonathan formally tonight; it was to be a great occasion. Kate seemed content with her future son-in-law, and about the suitability of a young man for their daughter she wasn't likely to be wrong.

It was another beautiful morning; this was one of the best summers in the South of England for many years. Gideon lingered over his breakfast, chatting to Kate about weddings and trousseaus and presents, his mind only half on the subject. He had the *Times* business section unopened near him, and caught a glimpse of the words "Rumors of Electronics New Age Takeover." Anything to do with electricity had a particular interest for him, and he began to read the opening paragraph.

"George. You haven't heard a word I've been saying," Kate protested.

"Yes, I have," said Gideon. "You've been saying that I'll have to ruin myself to see Penelope married." He grinned at her. "Well, if I have to be ruined I might as well enjoy the reason. Ring the office for me, love, and tell them I'll be walking this morning—along the Embankment if they need me."

"Walking?" Kate's gray eyes showed her astonishment.

"I want to think," said Gideon, and slapped his stomach. "If I have to think, I might as well keep my weight down at the same time."

As they laughed, there was a ring at the back door, and Kate got up saying, "That'll be the butcher." Gideon, alone, scanned the article. It was really a summary of speculations about one of the biggest of the electronic companies, telling him little, reaching the conclusion that Electronics New Age shares would probably reach a record high if production was maintained. Gideon, skimming, thinking about Boyd, suddenly saw a phrase, "recent series of blackouts," and quite suddenly his body stiffened and he gave the article all his attention.

"It is certain," he read, "that the recent series of blackouts in various London areas have had a serious effect on Electronics New Age and other companies, particularly those whose production has already been impeded by strike difficulties and internal differences. Future orders depend largely on keeping to a tight delivery schedule."

He got up and went into the passage for the nearest telephone, dialed his office, and asked for Hobbs. He was through immediately; Hobbs, being a widower, was often at his desk by seven in the morning.

"Anything more in about Boyd?" Gideon asked.

"Not yet," answered Hobbs.

"Seen the *Times* business section?"

"Yes."

"Electronics New Age Company?" Gideon asked.

"Yes—and the effect of the blackouts on the production and so the share values of allied and subsidiary companies," replied Hobbs.

"Should have known you wouldn't miss it," Gideon almost growled. "But we're very late on it, Alec. Get Osmington in as soon as you can."

"He's here."

"I'll be there in twenty minutes," Gideon promised. He put

167

down the receiver and saw Kate at the kitchen sink with a dish full of cellophane-covered stewing steak which she placed on the draining board. "Changed my mind about walking," Gideon said. "Malcolm gone to work yet?"

"No. I've told him to bring your car around."

Gideon stared, then laughed, gave her a hug, and went upstairs to put on his tie and jacket. Looking out of the window, he saw Malcolm driving the Humber with great care, and a boy of about the same age sitting next to him. Malcolm—driving. Malcolm—their youngest surviving child, the sixth. Out of the mists of memory came recollection of the seventh child, who had died in infancy when he, Gideon, had been forced to choose between duty and family. He had chosen duty, and for a long time he had feared that it would break his marriage. But the union had survived and Kate's bitterness had gradually died; the tensions between them had eased. He was happier, with Kate and at home, than he had ever been in his life.

Did Kate ever think back to those difficult days?

Of course she did; it was unavoidable.

What would happen to Penny and her Jonathan?

He hurried downstairs, shouted, "Bye, love!" and went out by the front doorway, Kate's voice echoing after him. Malcolm and his friend were standing beside the car, the engine of which was still running.

"Thanks, Son," Gideon said. "Morning, Willie." He got into the car and drove off slowly toward King's Road, putting on speed as he rounded the corner and found a gap in the traffic. He drove faster, goaded by a sense of great urgency, saw a policeman raise a hand, then lower it quickly as he recognized the Commander. He heard an ambulance siren, pulled in, let the ambulance pass, then drove after it along the road it cleared.

He was at the Yard in fourteen minutes.

"Put the car away," he said to a plainclothesman at the foot of the steps, and went up two at a time.

168

"Long time since Gee-Gee's been in such a hurry," the duty sergeant remarked. "Wonder what's up?"

Gideon went into Hobbs's office, where Hobbs was sitting at his desk opposite a short, rather humpbacked man with broad features and very thick lips. This was Superintendent Osmington, the C.I.D.'s expert on stocks and shares, market-rigging, share-pushing, and related offenses. He had huge, cow-like brown eyes and short hair which seemed to grow straight up from his pale forehead.

He sprang to his feet, nearly dropping a big book from his knees.

"Good morning, Commander!"

"Morning."

"Commander," said Hobbs, always punctilious when anyone else was with them.

"What have we got?" asked Gideon.

"I've a breakdown of companies which are having troubles and whose production has been affected by the blackouts," said Osmington. "It wasn't difficult; I simply rang the *Times*, and they had the information—in an article by a staff writer. There are eight in all."

"One in each of the affected areas?" asked Gideon.

"Yes, sir. Wembley, Slough, Uxbridge, Mitcham, Tottenham, Twickenham, Barking, and Greenwich. We're now making a list of the directors and major shareholders of the various companies, and the control of the companies."

"Any single control?"

Osmington looked at Hobbs.

"There's a pattern," Hobbs said. "Hibild, the building company, has a substantial holding in each. It has holdings in a great number of subsidiary companies, too—furniture manufacture, timber importers, cement, brick, and tile manufacturers, and bathroom and kitchen ware." He paused to allow Gideon to absorb all this, and went on: "The electrical manufacturing companies which had trouble all do a substantial share of their trade in manufacturing electrical equipment used in buildings—cable, wiring, electrical fittings, plugs—and also manufacture household goods such as washing machines, refrigerators, television, radio, and vacuum cleaners. They're all relatively small manufacturers compared with the giants like General Electric and English Electric, but when added together their output is very big."

Gideon sat on the corner of Hobbs's desk.

"Been doing research on this, Osmington?"

"I've been aware of it," the Superintendent answered cautiously. "It's just as well to know what's going on. I hadn't connected the power failures with any of these companies, but they're all obviously ripe for takeover by one of the bigger groups. The power cuts *could* have been deliberately aimed at them; there isn't the slightest evidence, sir, but the possibility is there."

"Yes. Anyone after them?"

"I've heard no rumors."

"Who would know?"

"The *Times* and the *Sunday Times*—and the *Financial Times*—all keep their ear to the ground," answered Osmington. "And they'll all help, if they can."

"Try them," ordered Gideon.

"Right."

"And check if John Boyd has any shares in any of these companies," said Gideon.

"That won't be too easy, and could take a lot longer, unless we know his broker," Osmington answered.

"Try," Gideon urged. "Let me or the Deputy Commander know of each development as it turns up."

"Very good, sir." Osmington heaved the heavy book, one of the two volumes of the *Stock Exchange Year Book*, onto the desk, and went out.

Gideon rubbed his chin, then put his left hand to his pocket and smoothed the big bowl of a pipe which he seldom smoked. Hobbs sat silent, reading from the notes in front of him. Suddenly Gideon spoke: "The one possibility we hadn't allowed for."

170

"You wanted to know whether the cuts had hurt any particular company," Hobbs reminded him. "You weren't happy about any of the more obvious theories."

"I'm not happy about this," Gideon retorted. After a pause, he went on, "Anything else in?" And before Hobbs could answer, he added, "What about the Morrison woman and George Jensen?"

"Jensen's dead," Hobbs told him flatly. "Mrs. Morrison's all right, though."

Gideon took his hand out of his pocket.

"I'm not sure it wouldn't have been better the other way round. Alec, we want someone who knows a lot about Hibild. Isn't that part of the Craven empire?"

"Yes," Hobbs answered.

"Who've we got?"

"I don't know that we've anybody who isn't already up to his neck," replied Hobbs. "But the headquarters are in the City, and the City Police are sure to have someone."

Gideon's eyes brightened.

"I'll talk to them," he said. "Good thought."

He went into his own office, sat down, and immediately asked for the Commissioner of the City of London Police, who was an old friend.

In two minutes, he was told, "The Commissioner is expected in during the next half hour, sir. Would you like to speak to someone else?"

"No," said Gideon. "Ask his secretary to call me when he's in."

"Very good, sir."

Gideon rang off, and looked with distaste at the files on his desk. This was one of the mornings when he found it difficult to get his mind off the major problem of the day, and it was no use pretending that he might be exaggerating the importance of it. There was no certainty of impending disaster, and yet he had that driving sense of urgency. He wished he knew more about the workings of the Stock Exchange and business —his was a general, not a specific, knowledge. He should

171

have thought of the City of London Police earlier—and, at the thought, laughed at himself. It was only about an hour and a half since he had first seen this aspect.

He stopped laughing.

"I should have seen it before," he said aloud. Then: "With a bit of luck, City will have Hibild at their fingertips."

The City of London Police, being the Force responsible for the City of London, would naturally be familiar with banking, insurance, the stock market, and all allied matters, conversant as they were with the head offices of the big banks and most of the insurance companies and shipping companies, and a great number of commercial and industrial firms.

Grimly, Gideon told himself that he might have been barking up the wrong tree, and so lost valuable time. At last, he began to open the files. Hobbs had made notes—and so had McAlistair, in some of them—and there were five Superintendents waiting to see or talk to him. He soon pushed the major investigation into the back of his mind and concentrated on the others.

20 Electronics New Age

One of the most important of the other cases was the fire at Mickle & Stratton, the murder of the night watchman—the cause of whose death had been burning, the autopsy report said—the disappearance of young George Jensen, and the death in a road accident of the youth's father. There was a note pinned to the front of the folder saying, "Superintendent Lemaitre is to be here at 12 noon." That was in about a half hour. Gideon dealt with all the others until he came upon a report from Richmond about the Morrison/Oliver case. It included two autopsy reports, one on the child Sheila, one on her murderer, Luke Oliver. The child had been brutally assaulted. There were marks on the mouth and lips, where sticking plaster had been placed to prevent her from crying out. *Could* any father be blamed for doing what he had?

Oliver had died of a bullet in the brain, another in the heart. So Morrison was a crack shot; he must have been absolutely calm when he had taken the gun from his pocket, absolutely cold-blooded. The prosecution would make a big issue of that; it had been a cold and calculated crime, not one committed in the grip of an overpowering emotion. Much would depend on the prosecuting counsel, of course.

The wife and mother, Lillian, was still in hospital, but could be released at any time. There was a note in Moore's handwriting: "She will go and stay with her mother until after the trial." And another note: "Child's funeral tomorrow. Oliver's Monday. I propose to attend each on behalf of the police."

173

Gideon nodded approval, put the file aside, stretched out for Honiwell's report from Epping, and opened the folder as the telephone bell rang. That would be the City Commissioner, he hoped, and picked up the receiver.

"Yes?"

"There's a Reverend Wilkinson on the line, sir, speaking from Truro."

After a prick of disappointment, Gideon said, "I'll speak to him." At the same time, he saw Honiwell's contribution for the morning: "No fresh developments to report." It was beginning to look as if they were not going to find their Epping Forest child killer. The speed with which Lillian Morrison had reported her child missing had certainly helped in that case.

"You're through."

"Is that Commander Gideon?" Wilkinson's voice was immediately recognizable.

"Yes."

"Commander, I've reason to believe that the youngest of the Entwhistle children has recollected incidents that could prove the existence of a close man friend—possibly a lover. I mean, her mother's, of course."

Gideon stalled. "Have you?" He was thinking, It's a job Honiwell could do well—go back over it, check everything that Golightly has done. Golightly, in Australia, would look down his nose if he ever found out what was planned— Good God! He, Gideon, was already accepting the case for probing deeper!

"Are you there, Commander?" Wilkinson sounded anxious.

"Yes. Mr. Wilkinson, you know that it is possible that any further investigation will only make the evidence more conclusive, but I understand your own and the children's position. I will have one of my senior officers discuss this with the foster parents, but you must understand it will be simply a discussion."

174

"That's all I ask for," said Wilkinson, his voice subdued. "Thank you, Commander. I'm very grateful."

As he spoke, the second telephone bell rang. Gideon said formally, "I can do no less," and put down one receiver as he picked up the other. His mind was as clear as it had ever been, and he felt not the slightest sense of being overpressed.

"Gideon."

"Good morning, George," said Sir Francis Rowbottom, the City Commissioner. "What can I do for you this morning?"

Gideon hesitated, needing only a moment to reorientate himself. The mental picture of Josiah Wilkinson soon faded, however, as that of a tall, dark-haired man took its place.

"Morning, Francis. Thanks for calling. Have you got a man who knows a lot about Hibild Limited?"

"Yes," answered the Commissioner, without hesitation.

Gideon, half prepared for a negative or a cautious answer, was taken aback, but Rowbottom filled in the gap.

"What do you want to know?"

"What kind of setup it is."

"Dangerously near a monopoly, in some of its aspects," answered Rowbottom. "I've been asked by the Monopolies Commission to get some information for them, and I never lose a chance of finding out what's going on in the City. I've had two men working on Hibild for three months—and on Sir Geoffrey Craven as well, for that matter. He's a modern Midas, if ever there was one."

"And I didn't know!" exclaimed Gideon.

"Should have told you," Rowbottom said. "We ought to meet more often and exchange odds and ends of information more frequently. What's your particular interest?"

"Have they been taking over any electrical companies lately?"

"They've been trying to," answered Rowbottom. "And they do it very cleverly. Individuals buy blocks of shares in the other companies; the actual firm doesn't appear. The

175

control is not always direct, but through individuals, and we haven't yet reached the stage where any private investor can be told what to do with his money. I can tell you one or two things which have made us open our eyes."

"Go on," said Gideon.

"Hibild has a director of one of London's biggest bookmaking companies on its Board—our old friend at Jackie Spratt's. Did you know that?"

"Well, well," said Gideon. "No, I did not."

"And Jackie Spratt's, Limited, has common directors and partners with many small stock and share brokers."

"Yes," Gideon said heavily. "I did know that."

"Something shaken you, George?" asked Rowbottom.

"Yes," repeated Gideon. He did not attempt to explain that he had recalled the disappearance of young George Jensen from an office in one of Jackie Spratt's branches—an office used independently by a stock and share broker. "Could you spare your two Hibild men for a few days?"

"Can't see why not," said Rowbottom. "I'll make sure they're not on anything else that matters. How urgent is this?"

"I think very urgent."

"The power cuts?" asked Rowbottom. "I hear you've been causing alarm and despondency among the powers that be!"

"Who talked?" asked Gideon.

"My brother-in-law is at Battersea Power Station," answered Rowbottom. "He's Chief of Security there."

"I remember," said Gideon, glad that there was such a simple explanation. "If I don't hear from you in half an hour, I'll expect your chaps over."

"Right," said Rowbottom.

Gideon rang off, sat back, and relaxed for the first time since he had seen the passing reference to the blackouts. He was becoming increasingly sure that he was on the right track; the whole affair had been too intricate for simple robbery.

How right was he to suspect John Boyd? And was "suspect" too strong a word?

He rang for Sabrina Sale but a younger, very pretty girl turned up.

"Miss Sale is with the Assistant Commissioner, sir—his secretary is away."

"Oh," said Gideon. "Well, I haven't much for you." He dictated a few letters and sent the girl off, realizing that he had been disappointed at the older woman's nonappearance. He couldn't be looking forward to his brief talks with her, could he? The odd, rather disturbing thought was pushed aside when there was a tap at the passage door.

Osmington came in, and not for the first time Gideon thought how like a Mongol he looked; but behind the unprepossessing face there was a very astute mind.

"I've more word about the companies affected, sir, and their major shareholders."

"Oh. Let's have it," said Gideon. "Come and sit down."

"Thank you, sir." Osmington had a sheaf of papers clipped together with a big black paper clip. "They are all loosely associated with the Electronics New Age company. They have a buying pool and a distribution pool, to keep expenses down and to compete better with the big boys. And there's been a lot of very quiet buying of their shares lately."

"Quiet buying?" asked Gideon.

"There's a pattern, very clearly marked now we have been alerted to it," Osmington answered. "Each of the factories has had troubles—strikes, breakdowns, loss of orders, some sabotage—"

"Sabotage!" echoed Gideon.

"Yes, sir. Goods almost ready for shipment have been damaged, machines have been damaged—nothing exceptional, but enough to be important in the aggregate. Each loss of production has shown in their results and their shares have dropped. Each company has lost orders to English competitors selling to major overseas markets—some to overseas competitors. And each loss of orders has resulted in the fall of shares for that particular company. They've always been picked up, but in small parcels, never enough to influence the price much. Then, when one firm has recovered, another in the group—"

"Group?"

"The loose association, I mean, sir—another firm in the group has run into trouble."

"Talked to them?" asked Gideon.

"To the secretary of Electronics New Age and the *Times* correspondent," answered Osmington. "You can rely on this information, sir. They were both together at the factory—the *Times* man's article worried them."

"I can understand why! Where's their main factory? Electronics New Age, I mean."

"Over at East Ham, sir," said Osmington.

Gideon sat very still.

"East Ham," he echoed. "Served by the New Bridge Power Station."

"That's right, sir."

Gideon was already getting to his feet, and his face was set and hard.

"And if there should be a power failure at Electronics New Age, what would happen?" he asked.

"At the moment it could be disastrous," answered Osmington. "They are working at full pressure on an order for an Australian company which has big orders to place for the future. Japanese and American competition is very fierce, and delivery is all-important. There are twenty computers to get ready for a ship leaving from Millwall Docks next Monday. They're paying double for all overtime, and working over the weekend. This is what the secretary is worried about —he wants to know where the *Times* correspondent got his information, wants to try to anticipate any kind of sabotage. It really could break them, sir—could bring the shares tumbling."

"How quickly?" demanded Gideon.

"Oh, in a matter of hours," Osmington said.

It was ten minutes after noon.

And at that moment, Sir Geoffrey Craven had a call from John Boyd.

"All set for one-forty-five," Boyd said. "You can rely on it."

And at that moment, Chief Superintendent Lemaitre of N.E. Division tapped perfunctorily on Gideon's door, and came in.

21 *Failure*

"George—" began Lemaitre, and then he saw Gideon's expression. "Gawd!"

"I'm going over to New Bridge," Gideon said. "We can talk on the way, if you like."

"Suits me," said Lemaitre. "What—"

Gideon's exchange telephone bell rang, and he stepped across and picked it up, and at the same time pressed the button for Hobbs. Lemaitre came a little farther into the room. Hobbs's door opened as Gideon lifted the receiver.

"Who is it?"

"This is the main hall, sir. Chief Inspector Wylie and Detective Sergeant Smith are asking for you."

"Send them along to me at once," ordered Gideon, and then to Hobbs: "They've come with a report on Hibild. Seen Osmington?"

"Yes—he's with me now."

"What do you make of it?"

"A cut at New Bridge could force Electronics New Age shares down to nothing."

"George—" began Lemaitre eagerly.

Gideon ignored him.

"Yes. But how can we stop it?"

"Let Boyd know you suspect it," Hobbs said.

"Commander!" Lemaitre broke in.

"Hold it, Lem. Alec, if we let Boyd know, and he's planning the cut, then he'd be able to bring the whole thing forward, and we wouldn't gain a thing."

"There's no certainty he is—" began Hobbs.

"We'll assume he is. It's Friday. The ship's due to sail on Monday at the morning tide, so the cut must come today if it's to affect delivery to the ship and bring the shares down."

Hobbs caught his breath.

"Yes."

"And he's in charge of security there," Gideon said, as if speaking to himself. "He knows the place inside out. What time is it?"

"Twenty past twelve."

"And dealing on the Stock Exchange stops at three. There's still a little time to maneuver in. How long will it take to get to New Bridge at this hour of the day, Lem?"

Lemaitre, who looked about to explode, made a funny little sound.

"Eh? Oh—an hour or more. George—"

"Just a minute, Lem. Alec—I'll take Piluski, and go by helicopter. Fix it." He strode to the desk and lifted the telephone, and as he did so there was a tap at the door, which opened to admit two men—one of whom he recognized— from the City Police. At that instant, he knew that if in fact there was the urgency he sensed, then he had no time to talk; yet no one else knew what he wanted to ask them.

Hobbs went out.

Gideon said into the telephone, "The Commissioner, at once." He held out a hand to the City men. "Gentlemen, how're you? Will you wait next door for a few minutes, please?" He raised a hand to Lemaitre, asking him to take them out of the room. By the time they had gone, Gideon began to wonder whether Scott-Marle was in his office, but at last the Commissioner spoke.

"Yes, Commander?"

"I think there is a very good chance that there will be a

181

power cut in E.F. Division area in the next hour or two," Gideon said. "I'm going to New Bridge Power Station by helicopter. I think the purpose might be to stop work at the Electronics New Age factory, and I haven't the faintest idea whether there's any way of supplying power from the grid to the factory if there is a breakdown at the power station. I hope I'm making myself clear, sir."

"Very clear. Go on."

"It's possible that if the grid authorities know there is going to be a cut in advance they can do more about it than if they have no warning. But no one is going to take much notice of me."

"I will do what I can," Scott-Marle promised at once.

"This *may* be a false alarm, sir."

"Then no harm will have been done."

Thank God for Scott-Marle, thought Gideon as he rang off.

"George—" Lemaitre, who had returned, began.

"For God's sake, Lem!" cried Gideon. "Can't you see—"

He broke off, aware for the first time of the expression on Lemaitre's face. Had it been any other man, he would have taken it to be simple exasperation, but there was an appeal in Lemaitre's eyes, an expression on his face which pleaded "Listen to me" in a curiously desperate way. Gideon, halfway to the door, stopped.

"All right," he said. "What is it?"

"Hibild," said Lemaitre.

"What about Hibild?"

"Those two City chaps—do they know"—Lemaitre hesitated, and then went on gustily—"Hibild has been trying to buy Easiphit Furniture out? Old Jeff Mickle won't sell; remember I told you? I put two and two together. It wouldn't be the first time Hibild has used some pretty risky tactics to get hold of a firm they want."

Gideon said very slowly, "Can you prove it wouldn't?"

"I don't know that I can prove it yet, but you should hear old Jeff Mickle," Lemaitre said. "There's another thing. We picked up a drunk in the Whitechapel Road last night, a man named Biddle. He was the man who ran old Jensen down. He's a stockbroker's clerk who went wrong years ago—odd-job man at the branch Kano managed. He keeps talking about an acid bath and there's a factory near Mill Lane where they make sulfuric acid. I'm sending some men round to take a look."

"Good," said Gideon. "Could be vital."

"And, George, Jeff Mickle—but you know all about Jeff if you've read my report this morning."

"I haven't seen a report from you this morning," Gideon said, feeling almost angry at this added delay; but it wasn't any good showing what he felt. "If you can get proof, even enough to justify us making inquiries about Hibild, you'll take a load off my mind."

"I'll fix it," Lemaitre said. "Want me to come with you, after all?"

"No."

The door opened, and Hobbs said, "The helicopter will be at the landing stage near Lambeth Bridge in ten minutes. I've a car ordered. Piluski's in N.E.—he'll meet you at the power station."

"Thanks," Gideon said. "I'll drive with Wylie and the other chap and tell them what I want on the way."

In the car, with lean Chief Inspector Wylie beside him and heavy, paunchy Detective Sergeant Smith next to the driver, Gideon said, "I want as many details as I can get of Hibild's subsidiary or associate companies and all details about share-holders in Hibild who are also big shareholders in other companies—and I want them quick. Really quick. How soon can you get them?"

"We'll need two or three days to get it all," Wylie answered. "But some of the information's on file already. We brought some files with us, as the Commissioner gave us a pretty good idea of what you're after."

"Give me the picture as you know it."

"Hibild has its tentacles everywhere," explained Wylie, quite dispassionately. "They have British, American, and Japanese capital, and they've developed overseas markets exclusive to them. They undercut competition to get new business in the newly emergent countries, as well as India, Pakistan, and South America—and they make long-term contracts for spare parts and maintenance."

The car turned around by the Houses of Parliament as Wylie broke off.

"Go on," Gideon urged.

"They also have tentacles in everything to do with building," Wylie told him. "Cement, steel, electrical equipment, furniture, and suchlike. They're probably the biggest civil-engineering organization in the world, certainly one of the biggest. And in order to evade the Monopolies Commission here and its equivalent in the U.S.A., they staff the boards with guinea pigs. I know how the Monopolies Commission works here," went on Wylie. "I doubt if Hibild, as at present constituted, comes within its range."

"So Craven's been really clever," remarked Gideon.

"It's obvious that he or others studied the problem carefully before taking steps. Until five years ago, Hibild was a small firm of civil-engineering contractors. Then Craven took over—"

"Took over?"

"Became managing director, with seventy-five per cent of the shares," stated Wylie.

"Where did he get his money then?"

"He brought in some foreign capital to get control, then bought the investors out. And did he spread fast! Hibild took nearly seven per cent of all metropolitan London building last year, and a much higher proportion of some provincial cities."

The car slowed down, just beyond Lambeth Bridge, nearly opposite the offices of the Ministry of Power. As it stopped,

184

Gideon was already moving to get out, and he glimpsed a helicopter on the big landing stage which had been built for both police and fire service use. The others followed and walked with him to the steps.

"Do you know any other major shareholders?" asked Gideon.

"Only the overseas ones are really big."

"Right. Get it all on paper; remember we may need to use it for more than a case for the Monopolies Commission to ponder. And thanks." He nodded, and stepped toward the helicopter, where the pilot, two policemen, and several engineers were standing.

A line of spectators, some with cameras poised, edged the parapet of the Embankment, and he heard a youth exclaim, "That's Gideon!"

"Who?"

"You know—the chief cop."

Gideon smiled grimly to himself as he stepped into the helicopter, crouching in the doorway, finding—as always to his surprise—plenty of room once he was inside. The pilot and one of the policemen climbed in after him.

"Where to, sir?" asked the pilot.

"New Bridge Power Station," Gideon said. "There's a big car park and with luck you'll be able to land there. If not, there's a small park between the power station and the river."

"I know the place, sir. The roof will do, if it's urgent."

"It's urgent all right." Gideon settled down as the engine started quivering, then became smooth as they took off. It was strange seeing the faces of the watchers getting smaller, seeing some of the little figures wave, finding himself on a level with and then above the roofs of buildings. There in front of him were the Houses of Parliament and beyond was a magnificent view along Whitehall as far as and beyond Trafalgar Square and Nelson's Column. The new buildings, square and oblong and somehow out of place, first dotted the skyline, then became part of the panorama, the green parks

185

and tree-clad land, the wide thoroughfares and the narrow lanes.

He had never seen London more beautiful, and for a few minutes the sun was directly behind him, showing everything in the best possible light. Slowly they turned east, and he could see the whole stretch of the river, the bridges, St. Paul's, and the Tower. He glanced behind him and saw the great stacks of the Battersea Power Station belching.

In five minutes or less they would see New Bridge; would its stacks be smoking? He reminded himself that he could still not be sure of the part John Boyd was playing in this; his feeling about the man was not much more than a hunch, at best an intelligent guess.

The radio crackled.

"For you, sir," the pilot said.

"Thanks." Gideon took what seemed like an ordinary telephone. "Gideon here."

"This is Hobbs," Hobbs said in his clear, distinctive voice; even without his noticeable deliberation, Gideon would have known that this call was of extreme importance. "I've just had a telephone report from Osmington." Hobbs paused, and Gideon sat very still. "John Boyd has given orders to his brokers to buy Electronics New Age in the last hour of business today, and again on Monday. And he's recently been buying shares of some of the companies affected by the blackout. He buys in small parcels but the total must be upward of a hundred thousand pounds. If Hibild takes over, that could be doubled in a few days."

Gideon said heavily, "So he *is* in it."

"No shadow of doubt," Hobbs said. "I've alerted the local Division, and the adjacent ones are throwing a cordon round New Bridge."

"Is Boyd there?"

"Yes. Everything appears to be normal."

"Thanks," Gideon said.

He rang off, and looked toward the east but was not yet close enough to pick out the New Bridge Power Station. He could see the Pool of London and the mass of shipping not only alongside the river front but in the great docks with their network of waterways, their huge warehouses, the railway lines, the enormous cranes. He could just make out Millwall Docks, where the S.S. *Walla Walla* was already loading and waiting for the computers from Electronics New Age.

"There's New Bridge, sir," the pilot said.

Gideon saw the two tall, slender stacks, smoke rising in enormous, rolling billows, darker than the smoke from Battersea. It was going straight up for perhaps fifty feet and then being carried sluggishly toward the northeast. The shapes of the nearby factories began to show up, including the long white building of Electronics New Age. It was still being fed, was still working at full pressure, which could make all the difference to its future.

Then the pilot said in a casual voice, "Isn't that smoke thinning, sir?"

Gideon narrowed his eyes.

"Is it?"

"Looks like it to me."

Gideon didn't speak, simply stared at the tall stacks and the smoke, watching the point where it actually left the chimney, his heart thumping, his left hand gripping the big, smooth bowl of his pipe.

It *was* lessening; there wasn't a doubt of it.

His heart felt like lead.

Suddenly, without a second's warning, the power supply to the area fed by New Bridge Power Station was cut off.

Suddenly, every machine driven by electricity, every tool, every light, every motor, stopped working.

Suddenly, there were urgent calls of alarm, emergency steps were taken in hospitals, dentists' drills stopped, boiling rings began to cool, refrigerators stopped.

In an area covering nearly a twelfth of London, all electric power died away.

In the Electronics New Age factory, there was a sense of

shock and horror among the skilled workers who had been working at rare pressure, and among the management and the white-collar staff.

"We'll never make it," the man Roscoe said.

"We might if it comes on within the hour."

"No—it will take too long to start up again. We've had it. We can't make that shipment." The general manager, slight and pale, looked absolutely defeated, utterly despairing.

John Boyd, in that first moment of disaster, grinned with animal ferocity and clapped his hands together with a tremendous bang. Then, the grin wiped off his face, he sprang toward the telescope and saw the control board of the distribution switches smoking and on fire.

22 Success

The helicopter landed with unexpected gentleness on the tarred surface at the far end of the New Bridge Power Station parking area. Two security guards and a dozen men came hurrying toward it as Gideon climbed out, Piluski among them. The gap between the two main buildings was filled with men, mostly in coveralls, and others were filing out of the generating house and the boilerhouses. One of the guards recognized Gideon.

"Good afternoon, sir."

"Where's Captain Boyd?"

"In the generating house," he said. "Over by the distribution panel. There's been a—"

Gideon did not wait to hear him finish but strode toward the entrance through which Boyd had taken him so recently. Piluski kept pace with him. Most of the workers were talking excitedly among themselves; only a few appeared to notice Gideon.

"It must have been a bomb."

"Wasn't the slightest warning."

"How many were hurt—any idea?"

"Must have been a dozen."

"*Hundred*, more like."

As yet, there was no sign of ambulances, fire engines, or injured people.

Gideon pushed his way past two security officers, into the enormous shed—and stood absolutely still. Over on the far

189

side, there were dozens of men on the floor, being attended by others. Huge doors were open and two ambulances stood, backs to the shed, and others were approaching. Over in a corner, a dozen men were spraying foam over the burning control board. Smoke was thick, and spreading fast. From outside there came the urgent clangor of a fire engine.

Boyd stood in the midst of the chaos, giving orders, in perfect control of himself and the situation. Security officers, first-aid men wearing the Order of St. John armlets, and nurses were moving among the injured as they were lifted onto stretchers and carried away. Men, obviously in charge, were giving orders at the turbogenerators, and Gideon realized something quite remarkable: there was hardly any noise.

Boyd moved around toward the other men.

"Are the boilerhouses all right?" one man asked.

"All heat's turned off," another said.

"Fuel feeds?"

"It's all under control."

"I'll believe that when I see it with my own eyes," Boyd growled.

A well-dressed, middle-aged man approached, with several others just behind him, and Boyd drew up and stopped growling. Gideon, some distance off, sensed that the newcomer was in authority here.

One of the security officers was close by, and Gideon asked, "Who's that?"

"The Controller, sir, Mr. Courtney."

Gideon nodded acknowledgment.

The Controller went straight to Boyd. He was lean and immaculate, pale, silver-haired; Boyd looked big and clumsy beside him—and belligerent. Nothing stopped over by the control board, but the two men and those about them formed a little oasis of stillness.

"Do you know what happened?" Courtney asked in a clipped voice.

190

"A magnetic bomb appears to have been fixed to the control board, sir," Boyd stated.

"*Appears* to have been?" Courtney's manner was scathing.

"No one was near the board at the moment of the explosion, sir. I have established that beyond all doubt."

"I had your assurance that nothing could go wrong."

"None of the most vulnerable points were attacked, sir."

"None of the—" Courtney began, then drew in a deep breath. He turned to the man who had asked about the boilerhouses. "Has every necessary action been taken, Mr. Sims?"

"Yes, sir. All generators have been stopped, all heaters—"

"I don't want details. Will you and Mr. Boardman make a personal check?"

"At once, sir."

Courtney turned back to Boyd.

"Do you know how many are injured?"

"Not precisely, sir."

"Are there any fatalities?"

"Yes, sir, but I don't know how many. There are also some serious injuries."

"Do you know who placed the bomb?"

"No, sir."

Gideon and Piluski moved a little nearer but were not noticed.

"Make it absolute priority to find out," Courtney ordered. He turned and looked at the scene of the explosion. Most of the injured were receiving attention now; several ambulances had gone and others were backing in. The flames were nearly out, but much of the control board and some of the machines near it were destroyed. He was obviously appalled, and when he turned back to Boyd there was a glitter in his eyes and for the first time his voice rose. "It is utterly unbelievable that you should have allowed such a disaster to happen."

Boyd glared—and Gideon moved another step forward.

"*I'm* not to blame!"

"You are the Chief Security Officer here and—"

"That's enough of that!" roared Boyd. "I can protect the plant against ordinary sabotage. I can't prevent bloody fanatics taking a chance of blowing themselves and the whole place up!"

Gideon, within a couple of yards, spoke for the first time.

"Captain Boyd, why have you instructed your brokers to buy Electronics New Age shares in the last hour of today's Stock Exchange business and again on Monday?"

It seemed a long time before anyone understood the significance of the question, and there was a puzzled silence before Courtney gasped, *"What?"*

"Would it be true to say that you anticipated this power failure, and made your personal plans accordingly?" inquired Gideon. His voice was even and his gaze steady.

Boyd's head turned slowly toward him, eyes glaring, lips parted, as if he could not believe what he had heard. Piluski moved up behind him, and it was evident that others had begun to understand what Gideon was implying. Gideon and Boyd were now face to face, with Courtney a yard away from them.

"And do you realize that whoever was responsible for the explosion here, whether directly or indirectly, will be charged with murder?" asked Gideon.

Boyd's mouth began to work, but he neither moved nor spoke.

It was a man in a blue coverall, at the back of the little crowd, who said in a shrill voice, "He inspected the control board himself half an hour ago! I saw him. He—"

Boyd roared, *"You bloody liar,"* and swung toward him, sweeping an arm round to push Gideon aside. Gideon grabbed his wrist and, before Boyd could prevent him, twisted the arm behind his back and forced it high. Boyd made one convulsive movement, then realized that if he

192

moved violently he would break his arm.

Gideon said roughly, "Now, let's have the truth. Why did you order your brokers to buy those shares? How did you know they would fall?"

"It's a lie! I did no such thing," Boyd gasped. Sweat poured down his forehead and into his eyes, and he made another convulsive movement to escape.

"I can prove that you did," Gideon stated simply, and saw handcuffs in Piluski's hand. He nodded and let Boyd go, but before the big man realized what was happening, the handcuffs were on his wrists.

Gideon thought, I hope to God Osmington was right.

As he spoke, as another ambulance snorted and drove off, a woman began to cry—low-pitched, heart-rending. Gideon, regaining his hold on Boyd, looked across at her. She was on her knees beside the body of a man on a stretcher, a man over whose face a stretcher-bearer was pulling a sheet.

The shrill-voiced man shouted from behind Gideon, "Murderer—bloody murderer!"

"Murderer, murderer!"

"It was Boyd!"

"Murderer!"

"Bloody murderer!"

The cry seemed to be taken up not by a dozen but by a hundred voices, and Gideon saw men approaching from all directions, some with spanners, some with hammers in their hands. Gideon felt Boyd's body begin to stiffen, felt him shivering—and then saw him twist his head around and heard him gasp.

"Get me out of here. Get me out! They'll bash me to pieces if you don't!"

Gideon, seeing the rage in the faces of men whose work-mates had just been killed or injured, seeing one man with

193

blood seeping from a wound in his forehead and another with a gash across his cheek, stepped onto one of the silent turbo-generator protectors. Piluski stood close by Boyd, with Courtney in front of him.

"Listen to me!" roared Gideon, his voice so powerful that men fifty yards away turned around. "My name is Gideon—Commander Gideon of Scotland Yard. We know who did this thing, we know why they did it, and you can be sure they will be tried and punished with the utmost rigor of the law."

He paused for a few tense seconds, and then ordered, "Now let us pass. Don't try to take the law into your own hands—let us pass—*now.*"

There was a deep hush as he stopped. Then slowly a path was made in the crowd, and he jumped down and went ahead. Boyd followed, Piluski brought up the rear, and no one tried to stop them.

On the way to the Yard, Boyd did not say a word.

During the flight back to Lambeth, however, a near miracle happened at Electronics New Age and to all the plants in the area. Power came back, through the grid. Machines began to hum and turn, and hope began to flow back, too. Scott-Marle had talked to good effect, and a major disaster was averted.

"We'll make that ship yet," Roscoe said, with lifting heart.

Gideon tapped at the door of the Commissioner's office late that afternoon, and as he opened the door Scott-Marle came toward him with his hand outstretched. Gideon, tired but very cheerful, for he knew now about the speed with which the current had been switched on, returned the strong pressure.

"If I'd only been half an hour earlier—" he began.

"Nonsense," interrupted Scott-Marle. "You worked miracles, George. Don't start reproaching yourself. I understand that the case against Boyd is virtually proved."

"No shadow of doubt," Gideon assured him. "A search at his flat revealed some fuse-holders of the kind used at New

Bridge, and some nitroglycerine and a time mechanism. The bomb was inside the fuse-holder. He doesn't even deny anything now. But he won't talk about his accomplices, and I doubt if he will. It will take us a long time to find out whether Sir Geoffrey Craven was involved, and there are other leaders we haven't yet identified—but the trouble as such is over."

"You wouldn't say that if you weren't sure," Scott-Marle said with confidence.

"I am sure, sir. Lemaitre has made a breakthrough in the arson case at Bethnal Green. Hibild was behind that, too, working through a man named Kano, Rupert Kano, who has vanished. A man employed by Kano has made a full confession. In all, at Kano's instigation, he started seven fires, forcing seven firms to sell out to subsidiaries of Hibild. The youth Jensen—" He broke off. "Do you know about him, sir?"

"Yes."

"He was paid to start the fire at Mickle & Stratton. He then seemed to have lost his nerve, so they killed him and pushed his body into a tank of sulfuric acid—the third such victim, according to our informant. I haven't yet been able to establish whether the betting firm of Jackie Spratt's is directly involved—there's no positive evidence, merely suspicion."

"What will you do about Sir Geoffrey Craven?"

"Question him, sir, and harass him continually. The City Police have been doing some undercover investigation for the Monopolies Commission—and we can get into the Hibild head office and examine their books without trouble. And we may soon be able to investigate his private affairs."

"Yes," Scott-Marle said. "We don't want any talk of one law for the rich and one for the poor."

"Can't stop the talk, sir," Gideon said philosophically. "There's one other case I'd like you to know about, one which has nothing at all to do with this."

"Yes?"

"A man named Entwhistle was convicted of the murder of his wife and sentenced to life imprisonment two years ago," said Gideon. "I think there's some doubt about the justice of the verdict, in view of recent information. I propose to put Honiwell onto that, quietly—he can do with a change from the Epping job. He can always go back to it if anyone comes under suspicion."

Scott-Marle said slowly, "I can imagine few things worse than being under a life sentence for a crime I didn't commit."

He made no other comment, but most certainly realized that Gideon was simply covering himself should the Assistant Commissioner disagree on the wisdom of reopening the investigation.

"Is there any news of Mrs. Morrison?" asked Scott-Marle.

"She's recovered from her attempted suicide and has gone to stay with her parents, sir. I'm preparing the papers for the Director of Public Prosecutions, about her husband; that's out of our hands now. I am sure we should try to make parents inform us much more quickly if a child is missing. I think we should ask the press and the broadcasting services to support us in a long-term campaign."

Scott-Marle said quietly, "Those crimes worry you more than any others, don't they?"

"I suppose they do," Gideon admitted. "Yes, I'm sure they do."

Soon afterward, he went along to his own office. There, faultlessly typed, were his own notes; Sabrina Sale was blessedly efficient. There, too, was Briggs's report on the arson case; somehow that had lost its urgency, and certainly there was nothing he could do about it tonight.

He put everything away, and left the office.

He went out of the Yard by a side entrance, and drove himself home. He stopped for a few minutes and looked at the mighty stacks of the Battersea Power Station. Tomorrow morning he would pass it again, on his way to briefing Osmington, Piluski, Honiwell, Lemaitre—a very self-satisfied Lemaitre—and would begin the long, long investigation into the Hibild crimes. He had no doubt of the eventual outcome,

196

only worry about the time it would take.

He started off again.

Fifteen minutes later, he was listening to the woeful strains of a prelude he couldn't name, very different in mood from the joyous playing he had last heard. He went, inquiringly, to see Kate in the kitchen.

"She's had a quarrel with Jonathan," Kate said as she washed flour off her fingers under a tap. "She'll be all right, George. Just pretend you've noticed nothing."

Very slowly, Gideon nodded. Soon he realized that Kate felt just as he did: relieved. Penny was so very young to marry.

Designed by Robert Freese
Set in 11 point Times Roman
Composed, printed and bound by The Haddon Craftsmen, Inc.
HARPER & ROW, PUBLISHERS, INCORPORATED